Gardens of the IMAGINATION

Gardens of the IMAGINATION

A Literary Anthology

Edited by Sophie Biriotti

Illustrations by Peter Malone

CHRONICLE BOOKS

SAN FRANCISCO

Library of Congress Cataloging-in-Publication Data:
Gardens of the imagination : a literary anthology /
edited by Sophie Biriotti ; illustrations by Peter Malone.
        p. cm.
    ISBN 0-8118-1884-5 (hc.)
    1. Gardens—Literary collections. 2. Gardening—
Literary collections. I. Biriotti, Sophie. II. Malone,
Peter, 1953–.
    PN6071.G27G38 1999
    808.8'0364—dc21   98-42838
                                       CIP

Printed in Hong Kong

Designed by PATRICIA EVANGELISTA

Distributed in Canada by Raincoast Books
8680 Cambie Street
Vancouver, British Columbia V6P 6M9

10 9 8 7 6 5 4 3 2 1

Chronicle Books
85 Second Street
San Francisco, California 94105

www.chroniclebooks.com

ACKNOWLEDGMENTS

Speak, Memory by Vladimir Nabokov, published by Weidenfeld and Nicolson, and Random House, Inc.

"From Hundred-Plant Garden to Three-Flavour Study" by Lu Hsun from *Dawn Blossoms Plucked at Dusk,* published by Foreign Languages Press, Peking and Wei Ming Society, Peking.

"The Garden of the Torah" from *Gabriel's Palace: Jewish Mystical Tales* by Howard Schwartz. Copyright © 1994 by Howard Schwartz. Used by permission of Oxford University Press, Inc.

Excerpt by Vita Sackville-West from *The Observer,* January 1950. Copyright © the Estate of Vita Sackville-West, reproduced by permission of Curtis Brown, London.

The Enchanted April by Elizabeth von Arnim, used by permission of Macmillan Publishers Ltd.

"Girl Gardening" from *Five Decades: Poems 1925–1970* by Pablo Neruda, English translation copyright © 1961 by Ben Belitt, used by permission of Grove/Atlantic, Inc.

Their Eyes Were Watching God by Zora Neale Hurston. Copyright © 1937 by Harper & Row Publishers, Inc. Renewed 1965 by John C. Hurston and Joel Hurston. Excerpt reprinted by permission of HarperCollins Publishers, Inc., and Virago Press/Little Brown & Co.

"The Baron in the Trees" from *Il Barone Rampante* by Italo Calvino, English translation by Archibald Coloquhan. Copyright © 1990

Palomar Srl © 1957 by Italo Calvino. All rights reserved. Reproduced by permission of The Wylie Agency (UK) Ltd. and HarperCollins Publishers Ltd.

"The Scarlet Flower" by Vsevolod Garshin from *The Penguin Book of Russian Short Stories,* edited by David Richards and translated by Peter Henry. Copyright © David Richards, published by Penguin Books.

"The Garden of Forking Paths" by Jorge Luis Borges, translated by Donald A. Yates, from *Labyrinths.* Copyright © 1962, 1964 by New Directions Publishing Corp. Reprinted by permission of New Directions Publishing Corp. and Laurence Pollinger Ltd.

"A Tale of Two Gardens" by Octavio Paz from *Collected Poems 1957–1987.* Copyright © 1986 by Octavio Paz and Eliot Weinburger. Reprinted by permission of New Directions Publishing Corp. and The Carcanet Press Limited.

"Bliss" by Peter Carey. Copyright © 1981 by Peter Carey. Reproduced by permission of the author c/o Rogers, Coleridge & White Ltd, 20 Powis Mews, London W11 1JN. "Bliss" is published by Faber & Faber (UK), Vintage (USA), and UQP (Australia).

Every effort has been made to trace and acknowledge the copyright owners of the texts included herein. If by chance there is an incorrect or missing credit, the editor and publisher apologize and will make necessary amendments in future editions.

TABLE OF CONTENTS

INTRODUCTION

IT SEEMS STRANGE at first sight that gardens could have fired the passionate imaginations of so many of the world's greatest writers. We associate gardens with genteel domestic pleasures; but this volume is a book of extremes. In it we learn that the garden is more than just a pleasant accommodation of man and nature. After all, a garden is the setting for the very first human drama. Eden, the ancestral home we are all destined never to recover, was simultaneously a place of safety and danger, innocence and temptation. The whole of human history since the Fall can be seen as the catalogue of mankind's vain attempts to re-create the paradise from which we were expelled.

Little wonder then that the garden figures so often in the collective imagination of various cultures: it is the perfect arena for the drama of human interaction; the richest and most resonant of metaphors. Real gardens are to be found in every one of the world's sprawling cities, silent testimonies to our struggle to recover that elusive moment of tranquillity and harmony with nature. And gardens of the imagination flourish among the leaves of our greatest books, bearing witness to the power of human thought.

Writing and gardening are related arts. The gardener labors over his patch of earth, scattering seeds, yanking out weeds. He tries to nourish growth from barren soil, or to impose order on teeming wilderness. His is the struggle to suffuse nature with human creativity, resisting decay and dissolution. Long after the gardener's death, the garden may bloom or sicken. To plan its continued prosperity requires a selfless, visionary devotion.

The writer's patch of earth is a lamp-lit rectangle of paper. Tirelessly, he strives to plant words in rows on the vellum. He frets that the words may not germinate; they may fall on the stony ground of the unreceptive ear; they may die choked by too rich a mixture of adjectives and ideas. But he must cling to hope: once planted, words may flourish in a later season into blooms gathered by an appreciative audience.

Writing has the power to re-create the majesty and harmony of the mythical garden. Coleridge's classic evocation of Kubla Khan's paradise on earth constructs a garden out of pure syllabic energy—a garden fashioned out of poetry. A youthful piece by Vladimir Nabokov offers a contemporary counterpart in prose, with an intoxicating account of his summers spent butterfly-catching among the darkening lilacs of a Russian garden. The paradise recollected here includes an almost erotic account of "sugaring" the trees to attract unearthly beauties.

What Nabokov recollects is the enchantment of the garden seen through the eyes of a child. The phenomenon has universal appeal: the Chinese writer Lu Hsun writes of the garden as a place of mysteries and adult danger—where tubers shaped like men and snake women might linger in the long grass. And the British mathematician Lewis Carroll writes of a garden where the flowers come alive and assail his heroine Alice with their hilarious logic. Flowers, it seems, are always animate: but they tend to fall asleep on flower beds made too comfortable.

The wonder of the garden is its ability to restore. Nature renews itself as if by magic, and gardens can heal and transform with miraculous effect. "The Garden of the Torah" returns an overworked Rabbi Shmelke to full capacity in his sleep, and Frances Hodgson Burnett's sulky heroine Mary Lennox is metamorphosed into a resourceful and active child when she discovers the miracle of new and tentative growth in the matted, desiccated wilderness of *The Secret Garden*.

More than just a setting for human interaction, the garden is the ultimate in rich and versatile metaphors. Nowhere is this more appropriate than in the field of love and human passion. This association stretches across the ages: the Song of Solomon has long been admired as a jewelled miniature of ancient Middle-Eastern exoticism: is the garden it describes really a garden, or a woman? In our own era, Zora Neale Hurston's *Their Eyes Were Watching God* shows fecundity in full bloom, with the teenage African American heroine yearning to be part of nature's dance. Italo Calvino, meanwhile, offers a delicious play on the idiom of the garden of courtly love, recasting it as a place of outlandish exoticism and hilarious aloofness.

Enchantment, healing, and love: these are the themes that liken every garden to paradise. But even paradise had its darker side, lurking in the undergrowth. The ultimate description of it is John Milton's evocation of Satan, whose hymn of praise to Eve occasions the gradual weakening of her resistance and is a masterpiece of rhetoric. The garden is the scene of the ultimate betrayal and loss. Tennyson's *Maud* speaks of the tragedy of losing. Hawthorne, meanwhile, weaves a complex narrative thread of treachery and deceit.

The garden has the most extraordinary effect on the human mind. In Garshin's "The Scarlet Flower," a patient, recovering in an asylum, attributes mystical significance to all he encounters. In his fevered imaginings, the garden to which he is assigned takes on the deadly aspect of horror. Jorge Luis Borges, the Argentine literary trickster, takes us still further into the garden of the mind in a metaphysical whodunit of dazzling complexity. In it, the garden becomes a labyrinth in which all temporal possibilities and outcomes are possible.

The last two pieces in the book render the relationship between man and garden more poignantly. In Peter Carey's "Bliss," a man endures a double death and finds that we are all part of the vicissitudes of the universal garden. Octavio Paz too takes up this metaphor for life and death. Our lives, he muses, are merely a passage through a garden:

> A garden is not a place:
> it is a passage,
> a passion.
> We don't know where we're going,
> to pass through is enough,
> to pass through is to remain:

This is an anthology in the original sense of the word—a "bouquet of choice flowers" hand-picked from the garden of our collective imagining. Each of the extracts offered in this volume has been chosen because of its inspirational quality, taking us to the opened space of the writer's creativity. Peter Malone's exquisite illustrations lend visual splendor to the majesty of the words. Whether the reader seeks quiet reflection, fiery inspiration, or simply the evocation of nature's bounty, abiding for a while among the leaves of this volume will open a vista to the gardens of the imagination.

Gardens of PARADISE

THE GARDEN OF EDEN

Genesis 2:4–17

4 These *are* the generations of the heavens and of the earth when they were created, in the day that the LORD GOD made the earth and the heavens,

5 And every plant of the field before it was in the earth, and every herb of the field before it grew: for the LORD GOD had not caused it to rain upon the earth, and *there was* not a man to till the ground.

6 But there went up a mist from the earth, and watered the whole face of the ground.

7 And the LORD GOD formed man *of* the dust of the ground, and breathed into his nostrils the breath of life; and man became a living soul.

8 And the LORD GOD planted a garden eastward in Eden; and there he put the man whom he had formed.

9 And out of the ground made the LORD GOD to grow every tree that is pleasant to the sight, and good for food; the tree of life also in the midst of the garden, and the tree of knowledge of good and evil.

10 And a river went out of Eden to water the garden; and from thence it was parted, and became into four heads.

11 The name of the first *is* Pison: that *is* it which compasseth the whole land of Havilah, where *there is* gold;

12 And the gold of that land *is* good: there *is* bdellium and the onyx stone.

13 And the name of the second river *is* Gihon: the same *is* it that compasseth the whole land of Ethiopia.

14 And the name of the third river *is* Hiddekel: that *is* it which goeth toward the east of Assyria. And the fourth river *is* Euphrates.

15 And the LORD GOD took the man, and put him into the garden of Eden to dress it and to keep it.

16 And the LORD GOD commanded the man, saying, Of every tree of the garden thou mayest freely eat:

17 But of the tree of knowledge of good and evil, thou shalt not eat of it: for in the day that thou eatest thereof thou shalt surely die.

THE HANGING GARDENS
OF BABYLON

Myth

ABOUT THE 5TH CENTURY BC the Babylonian king Nebuchadnezzar married the Median princess Amytis. She was soon homesick for the green hills and trees of her native land. To gratify her, the king built a huge structure 400 feet square on the west bank of the River Euphrates. In the crowded city of Babylon it rose as a pyramid to the height of 100 feet and was one of the seven wonders of the world.

It is said that the gardens were lined with cement and great sheets of lead to protect the walls of the building from the moisture which seeped from above. Each terrace cascaded with blooms: shrubs and flowers which delighted Babylon with their impossible colors and beguiling perfumes. The earth gave forth unprecedented lushness, and every tree grew tall and strong, every plant a wonder of the natural world.

KUBLA KHAN

Samuel Taylor Coleridge

IN XANADU did Kubla Khan
A stately pleasure dome decree:
Where Alph, the sacred river, ran
Through caverns measureless to man
 Down to a sunless sea.
So twice five miles of fertile ground
With walls and towers were girdled round:
And there were gardens bright with sinuous rills,
Where blossomed many an incense-bearing tree;
And here were forests ancient as the hills,
Enfolding sunny spots of greenery.

But oh! that deep romantic chasm which slanted
Down the green hill athwart a cedarn cover!
A savage place! as holy and enchanted
As e'er beneath a waning moon was haunted
By woman wailing for her demon lover!
And from this chasm, with ceaseless turmoil seething,
As if this earth in fast thick pants were breathing,
A mighty fountain momently was forced:
Amid whose swift half-intermitted burst
Huge fragments vaulted like rebounding hail,
Or chaffy grain beneath the thresher's flail:
And 'mid these dancing rocks at once and ever

It flung up momently the sacred river.
Five miles meandering with a mazy motion
Through wood and dale the sacred river ran,
Then reached the caverns measureless to man,
And sank in tumult to a lifeless ocean:
And 'mid this tumult Kubla heard from far
Ancestral voices prophesying war!

The shadow of the dome of pleasure
Floated midway on the waves;
Where was heard the mingled measure
From the fountain and the caves.
It was a miracle of rare device,
A sunny pleasure dome with caves of ice!

A damsel with a dulcimer
In a vision once I saw:
It was an Abyssinian maid,
And on her dulcimer she played,
Singing of Mount Abora.
Could I revive within me
Her symphony and song,
To such a deep delight 'twould win me,
That with music loud and long,
I would build that dome in air,
That sunny dome! those caves of ice!
And all who heard should see them there,
And all should cry, Beware! Beware!
His flashing eyes, his floating hair!
Weave a circle round him thrice,
And close your eyes with holy dread,
For he on honey-dew hath fed,
And drunk the milk of Paradise.

SPEAK, MEMORY

Vladimir Nabokov

THAT SUMMER I had been collecting assiduously on moonless nights, in a glade of the park, by spreading a bedsheet over the grass and its annoyed glow-worms, and casting upon it the light of an acytelene lamp (which, six years later, was to shine on Tamara). Into that arena of radiance, moths would come drifting out of the solid blackness around me, and it was in that manner, upon that magic sheet, that I took a beautiful *Plusia* (now *Phytometra*) which, as I saw at once, differed from its closest ally by its mauve-and-maroon (instead of golden-brown) forewings, and narrower bractea mark and was not recognizably figured in any of my books. I sent its description and picture to Richard South, for publication in *The Entomologist.* He did not know it either, but with the utmost kindness checked it in the British Museum collection—and found it had been described long ago as *Plusia excelsa* by Kretschmar. I received the sad news, which was most sympathetically worded (" . . . should be congratulated for obtaining . . . very rare Volgan thing . . . admirable figure . . . ") with the utmost stoicism; but many years later, by a pretty fluke (I know I should not point out these plums to people), I got even with the first discoverer of my moth by giving his own name to a blind man in a novel.

Let me also evoke the hawkmoths, the jets of my boyhood! Colors would die a long death on June evenings. The lilac shrubs in full bloom before which I stood, net in hand, displayed clusters of a fluffy gray in the dusk—the ghost of purple. A moist young moon hung above the mist of a neighboring meadow. In many a garden have I stood thus in later years—in Athens, Antibes, Atlanta—but never have I waited

with such a keen desire as before those darkening lilacs. And suddenly it would come, the low buzz passing from flower to flower, the vibrational halo around the stream-lined body of an olive and pink Hummingbird moth poised in the air above the corolla into which it had dipped its long tongue. Its handsome black larva (resem-bling a diminutive cobra when it puffed out its ocellated front segments) could be found on dank willow herb two months later. Thus every hour and season had its delights. And, finally, on cold, or even frosty, autumn nights, one could sugar for moths by painting tree trunks with a mixture of molasses, beer, and rum. Through the gusty blackness, one's lantern would illumine the stickily glistening furrows of the bark and two or three large moths upon it imbibing the sweets, their nervous wings half open butterfly fashion, the lower ones exhibiting their incredible crimson silk from beneath the lichen-gray primaries. *"Catocala adultera!"* I would triumphantly shriek in the direction of the lighted windows of the house as I stumbled home to show my captures to my father.

Gardens of ENCHANTMENT

FROM HUNDRED-PLANT GARDEN TO
THREE-FLAVOUR STUDY

Lu Hsun

BEHIND OUR HOUSE was a great garden known in our family as Hundred-Plant Garden. It has long since been sold, together with the house, to the descendants of Chu Hsi; and the last time I saw it, already seven or eight years ago, I am pretty sure there were only weeds growing there. But in my childhood it was my paradise.

I need not speak of the green vegetable plots, the slippery stone coping round the well, the tall honey-locust tree, or the purple mulberries. Nor need I speak of the long shrilling of the cicadas among the leaves, the fat wasps couched in the flowering rape, or the nimble skylarks who suddenly soared straight up from the grass to the sky. Just the foot of the low mud wall around the garden was a source of unfailing interest. Here field crickets droned away while house crickets chirped merrily. Turning over a broken brick, you might find a centipede. There were stinkbeetles as well, and if you pressed a finger on their backs they emitted puffs of vapour from their rear orifices. Milkwort interwove with climbing fig which had fruit shaped like the calyx of a lotus, while the milkwort had swollen tubers. Folk said that some of these had human shapes and if you ate them you would become immortal, so I kept on pulling them up. By uprooting one I pulled out those next to it, and in this way destroyed part of the mud wall, but I never found a tuber shaped like a man. If you were not afraid of thorns you could pick raspberries too, like clusters of little coral beads, sweet yet tart, with a much finer colour and flavour than mulberries.

I did not venture into the long grass, because a huge brown snake was said to inhabit the garden.

Mama Chang had told me a story:

Once upon a time a scholar was staying in an old temple to study. One evening while enjoying the cool of the courtyard he heard someone call his name. Responding he looked round and saw, over the wall, the head of a beautiful woman. She smiled, then disappeared. He was very pleased, till the old monk who came to chat with him each evening discovered what had happened. Detecting an evil influence on his face, he declared that the scholar must have seen the Beautiful-Woman Snake—a monster with a human head and snake's body who was able to call a man's name. If he answered, the snake would come that night to devour him.

The scholar was nearly frightened to death, of course; but the old monk told him not to worry and gave him a little box, assuring him that if he put this by the pillow he could go to sleep without fear.

But though the scholar did as he was told, he could not sleep—and that is hardly surprising. At midnight, to be sure, the monster came! There sounded a hissing and rustling, as if of wind and rain, outside the door. Just as he was shaking with fright, however—whizz—a golden ray streaked up from beside his pillow. Then outside the door utter silence fell, and the golden ray flew back once more to its box.

And after that? After that the old monk told him that this was a flying centipede which could suck out the brains of a snake—the Beautiful-Woman Snake had been killed by it.

The moral of this was: If a strange voice calls your name, on no account answer.

This story brought home to me the perils with which human life is fraught. When I sat outside on a summer night I often felt too apprehensive to look at the wall, and longed for a box with a flying centipede in it like the old monk's. This was often in my thoughts when I walked to the edge of the long grass in Hundred-Plant Garden. To this day I have never got hold of such a box, but neither have I encountered the brown snake or Beautiful-Woman Snake. Of course, strange voices often call my name, but they have never proved to belong to Beautiful-Woman Snakes.

In winter the garden was relatively dull; as soon as it snowed, though, that was a different story. Imprinting a snowman (by pressing your body on the snow) or building snow Buddhas required appreciative audiences; and since this was a deserted garden where visitors seldom came, such games were out of place here. I was therefore reduced to catching birds.

THE GARDEN
OF LIVE FLOWERS

Lewis Carroll

"I SHOULD SEE the garden far better," said Alice to herself, "if I could get to the top of that hill; and here's a path that leads straight to it—at least, no, it doesn't do *that*"—(after going a few yards along the path, and turning several sharp corners), "but I suppose it will at last. But how curiously it twists! It's more like a corkscrew than a path! Well, *this* turn goes to the hill, I suppose—no, it doesn't! This goes straight back to the house! Well then, I'll try it the other way."

And so she did: wandering up and down, and trying turn after turn, but always coming back to the house, do what she would. Indeed, once, when she turned a corner rather more quickly than usual, she ran against it before she could stop herself.

"It's no use talking about it," Alice said, looking up at the house and pretending it was arguing with her. "I'm *not* going in again yet. I know I should have to get through the Looking-glass again—back into the old room—and there'd be an end of all my adventures!"

So, resolutely turning her back upon the house, she set out once more down the path, determined to keep straight on till she got to the hill. For a few minutes all went on well, and she was just saying "I really *shall* do it this time"—when the path gave a sudden twist and shook itself (as she described it afterwards), and the next moment she found herself actually walking in at the door.

"Oh, it's too bad!" she cried. "I never saw such a house for getting in the way! Never!"

However, there was the hill full in sight, so there was nothing to be done but

start again. This time she came upon a large flower-bed, with a border of daisies, and a willow-tree growing in the middle.

"O Tiger-lily!" said Alice, addressing herself to one that was waving gracefully about in the wind, "I *wish* you could talk!"

"We *can* talk," said the Tiger-lily, "when there's anybody worth talking to."

Alice was so astonished that she couldn't speak for a minute: it quite seemed to take her breath away. At length, as the Tiger-lily only went on waving about, she spoke again, in a timid voice—almost in a whisper. "And can *all* the flowers talk?"

"As well as *you* can," said the Tiger-lily. "And a great deal louder."

"It isn't manners for us to begin, you know," said the Rose, "and I really was wondering when you'd speak! Said I to myself, 'Her face has got *some* sense in it, though it's not a clever one!' Still, you're the right colour, and that goes a long way."

"I don't care about the colour," the Tiger-lily remarked. "If only her petals curled up a little more, she'd be all right."

Alice didn't like being criticized, so she began asking questions. "Aren't you sometimes frightened at being planted out here, with nobody to take care of you?"

"There's the tree in the middle," said the Rose. "What else is it good for?"

"But what could it do, if any danger came?" Alice asked.

"It could bark," said the Rose.

"It says 'Bough-wough!'" cried a Daisy. "That's why its branches are called boughs!"

"Didn't you know *that?*" cried another Daisy. And here they all began shouting together, till the air seemed quite full of little shrill voices. "Silence, every one of you!" cried the Tiger-lily, waving itself passionately from side to side, and trembling with excitement. "They know I can't get at them!" it panted, bending its quivering head towards Alice, "or they wouldn't dare to do it!"

"Never mind!" Alice said in a soothing tone, and, stooping down to the daisies, who were just beginning again, she whispered "If you don't hold your tongues, I'll pick you!"

There was silence in a moment, and several of the pink daisies turned white.

"That's right!" said the Tiger-lily. "The daisies are worst of all. When one speaks, they all begin together, and it's enough to make one wither to hear the way they go on!"

"How is it you can all talk so nicely?" Alice said, hoping to get it into a better temper by a compliment. "I've been in many gardens before, but none of the flowers could talk."

"Put your hand down, and feel the ground," said the Tiger-lily. "Then you'll know why."

Alice did so. "It's very hard," she said; "but I don't see what that has to do with it."

"In most gardens," the Tiger-lily said, "they make the beds too soft—so that the flowers are always asleep."

This sounded a very good reason, and Alice was quite pleased to know it. "I never thought of that before!" she said.

"It's *my* opinion that you never think at all," the Rose said, in a rather severe tone.

"I never saw anybody that looked stupider," a Violet said, so suddenly, that Alice quite jumped; for it hadn't spoken before.

"Hold *your* tongue!" cried the Tiger-lily. "As if *you* ever saw anybody! You keep your head under the leaves, and snore away there, till you know no more what's going on in the world, than if you were a bud!"

"Are there any more people in the garden besides me?" Alice said, not choosing to notice the Rose's last remark.

"There's one other flower in the garden that can move about like you," said the Rose. "I wonder how you do it—" ("You're always wondering," said the Tiger-lily), "but she's more bushy than you are."

"Is she like me?" Alice asked eagerly, for the thought crossed her mind, "There's another little girl in the garden, somewhere!"

"Well, she has the same awkward shape as you," the Rose said: "but she's redder—and her petals are shorter, I think."

"They're done up close, like a dahlia," said the Tiger-lily: "not tumbled about, like yours."

"But that's not *your* fault," the Rose added kindly. "You're beginning to fade, you know—and then one can't help one's petals getting a little untidy."

Gardens of TRANSFORMATION

THE GARDEN OF THE TORAH

Howard Schwartz

REB SHMELKE TRIED to stay awake all the time to study Torah. He held a candle in one hand, so that if he fell asleep the flame would wake him when the candle burned down. Reb Elimelech once visited Reb Shmelke and noticed this, and he told him that it was imperative that he rest. He said: "You can serve God in many ways, even in your sleep."

Reb Shmelke took these words to heart and agreed to lie down on a couch in his study. He fell into a very deep sleep, and he had a dream in which he was traveling through a cave with Reb Elimelech, and Elimelech was holding a torch in his hand that illumined the cave from one end to the other. They traveled through this cave for years, but as they never stopped discussing the Torah, the time flew by for them, so the years seemed like hours and the hours like minutes.

At last they came to the other end of the cave and stepped out into a beautiful garden, with olives and dates so large that they shone like precious gems. Together with Reb Elimelech, Reb Shmelke explored every corner of that garden, and Reb Shmelke never wanted to leave it, for everywhere he went he saw the Name of God before him. In this way he recognized that they had reached the Garden of the Torah, which is also known as *Gan Eden,* the Garden of Eden.

Meanwhile, Reb Shmelke remained asleep. Everyone knew he was exhausted, so no one worried when he slept for a full day without waking. But by the end of the second day they were concerned, and by the end of the third day they were quite anxious. But no matter what they tried, they could not awaken him.

At the end of the seventh day they were desperate, and they begged Reb Elimelech to try to wake him, for they knew that no one else could succeed. Now all this time Reb Elimelech had not seemed the least bit worried about Reb Shmelke, but since they had asked for his help, he led them into Shmelke's study and placed his hand over the *mezzuzah.*

At that moment, in his dream, Reb Shmelke and Reb Elimelech had found their way to the gate at the entrance of that garden. And there, on the doorpost, Reb Shmelke had seen a *mezzuzah.* He looked at the *mezzuzah,* which seemed very familiar, and realized it looked exactly like the one on the door of his study. At that instant the Name of God, which had been before him all the time he had been in that garden, disappeared, and Reb Shmelke gasped and opened his eyes. That is when he found himself lying on the couch in his study, with a dozen bystanders watching him.

At first Shmelke was grieved to have been awakened out of that perfect dream and forced to leave that immortal garden. But when he learned how Elimelech had placed his hand over the *mezzuzah,* he understood that he had been permitted to remain in that Paradise, the Garden of the Torah, as long as possible, and now he had to return to the world of men. For when Reb Elimelech had placed his hand over the *mezzuzah,* he had covered the Name of God, and that is why it had vanished for Reb Shmelke. But now that he was awake he continued to see the Name of God before him, and this lasted all the days of his life. Reb Shmelke smiled at Reb Elimelech and said: "If only you had been with me!" And Reb Elimelech replied: "But of course I was!"

The next day, when Reb Shmelke preached to the congregation about the crossing of the Red Sea, it was said that the lapping of the waves could be felt, and the sound of the waters filled their ears. For that long sleep had restored him to his full powers, which rarely have been seen in this world.

THE SECRET GARDEN

Frances Hodgson Burnett

IT WAS THE SWEETEST, most mysterious-looking place anyone could imagine. The high walls which shut it in were covered with the leafless stems of climbing roses, which were so thick that they were matted together. Mary Lennox knew they were roses because she had seen a great many roses in India. All the ground was covered with grass of a wintry brown, and out of it grew clumps of bushes which were surely rose-bushes if they were alive. There were numbers of standard roses which had so spread their branches that they were like little trees. There were other trees in the garden, and one of the things which made the place look strangest and loveliest was that climbing roses had run all over them and swung down long tendrils which made light swaying curtains, and here and there they had caught at each other or at a far-reaching branch and had crept from one tree to another and made lovely bridges of themselves. There were neither leaves nor roses on them now, and Mary did not know whether they were dead or alive, but their thin grey or brown branches and sprays looked like a sort of hazy mantle spreading over everything, walls, and trees, and even brown grass, where they had fallen from their fastenings and run along the ground. It was this hazy tangle from tree to tree which made it look so mysterious. Mary had thought it must be different from other gardens which had not been left all by themselves so long; and, indeed, it was different from any other place she had ever seen in her life.

"How still it is!" she whispered. "How still!"

Then she waited a moment and listened at the stillness. The robin, who had

flown to his tree-top, was still as all the rest. He did not even flutter his wings; he sat without stirring, and looked at Mary.

"No wonder it is still," she whispered again. "I am the first person who has spoken in here for ten years."

She moved away from the door, stepping as softly as if she were afraid of awakening someone. She was glad that there was grass under her feet and that her steps made no sounds. She walked under one of the fairy-like arches between the trees and looked up at the sprays and tendrils which formed them.

"I wonder if they are all quite dead," she said. "Is it all a quite dead garden? I wish it wasn't."

If she had been Ben Weatherstaff she could have told whether the wood was alive by looking at it, but she could only see that there were only grey or brown sprays and branches, and none showed any signs of even a tiny leaf-bud anywhere.

But she was *inside* the wonderful garden, and she could come through the door under the ivy any time, and she felt as if she had found a world all her own.

The sun was shining inside the four walls and the high arch of blue sky over this particular piece of Misselthwaite seemed even more brilliant and soft than it was over the moor. The robin flew down from his tree-top and hopped about or flew after her from one bush to another. He chirped a good deal and had a very busy air, as if he were showing her things. Everything was strange and silent, and she seemed to be hundreds of miles away from anyone, but somehow she did not feel lonely at all. All that troubled her was her wish that she knew whether all the roses were dead, or if perhaps some of them had lived and might put out leaves and buds as the weather got warmer. She did not want it to be a quite dead garden. If it were a quite alive garden, how wonderful it would be, and what thousands of roses would grow on every side?

Her skipping-rope had hung over her arm when she came in, and after she had walked about for a while she thought she would skip round the whole garden, stopping when she wanted to look at things. There seemed to have been grass paths here and there, and in one or two corners there were alcoves of evergreen with stone seats or all moss-covered flower-urns in them.

As she came near the second of these alcoves she stopped skipping. There had once been a flower-bed in it, and she thought she saw something sticking out of the black earth—some sharp little pale green points. She remembered what Ben Weatherstaff had said, and she knelt down to look at them.

"Yes, they are tiny growing things and they *might* be crocuses or snowdrops or daffodils," she whispered.

She bent very close to them and sniffed the fresh scent of the damp earth. She liked it very much.

"Perhaps there are some other ones coming up in other places," she said. "I will go all over the garden and look."

She did not skip, but walked. She went slowly and kept her eyes on the ground. She looked in the old border-beds and among the grass, and after she had gone round, trying to miss nothing, she had found ever so many more sharp, pale green points, and she had become quite excited again.

"It isn't a quite dead garden," she cried out softly to herself. "Even if the roses are dead, there are other things alive."

She did not know anything about gardening, but the grass seemed so thick in some of the places where the green points were pushing their way through that she thought they did not seem to have room enough to grow. She searched about until she found a rather sharp piece of wood and knelt down and dug and weeded out the weeds and grass until she made nice little clear places around them.

"Now they look as if they could breathe," she said, after she had finished with the first ones. "I am going to do ever so many more. I'll do all I can see. If I haven't time today I can come tomorrow."

She went from place to place, and dug and weeded, and enjoyed herself so immensely that she was led on from bed to bed and into the grass under the trees. The exercise made her so warm that she first threw her coat off, and then her hat, and without knowing it she was smiling down on to the grass and the pale green points all the time.

The robin was tremendously busy. He was very much pleased to see gardening begun on his own estate. He had often wondered at Ben Weatherstaff. Where gardening is done all sorts of delightful things to eat are turned up with the soil. Now here was this new kind of creature who was not half Ben's size and yet had the sense to come into his garden and begin at once.

FROM A COLUMN IN *THE OBSERVER,*
JANUARY 1950

Vita Sackville-West

I HOPE YOU WILL SURVEY a low sea of grey clumps of foliage, pierced here and there with tall white flowers. I visualize the white trumpets of dozens of Regale lilies, grown three years ago from seed, coming up through the grey of southern-wood and artemisia and cotton-lavender, with grey-and-white edging plants such as *Dianthus* 'Mrs Sinkins,' and the silvery mats of *Stachys lanata,* more familiar and so much nicer under its English name of Rabbits' Ears or Saviour's Flannel. There will be white pansies, and white peonies, and white irises with their grey leaves . . . at least, I hope there will be all these things. I don't want to boast in advance about my grey, green, and white garden. It may be a terrible failure. I wanted only to suggest that such experiments are worth trying, and that you can adapt them to your own taste and your own opportunities.

All the same, I cannot help hoping that the great ghostly barn-owl will sweep silently across a pale garden, next summer in the twilight—the pale garden that I am now planting, under the first flakes of snow.

THE ENCHANTED APRIL

Elizabeth von Arnim

ALL DOWN THE STONE STEPS on either side were periwinkles in full flower, and she could now see what it was that had caught at her the night before and brushed, wet and scented, across her face. It was wistaria. *Wistaria and sunshine...* she remembered the advertisement. Here indeed were both in profusion. The wistaria was tumbling over itself in its excess of life, its prodigality of flowering; and where the pergola ended the sun blazed on scarlet geraniums, bushes of them, and nasturtiums in great heaps, and marigolds so brilliant that they seemed to be burning, and red and pink snapdragons, all outdoing each other in bright, fierce colour. The ground behind these flaming things dropped away in terraces to the sea, each terrace a little orchard, where among the olives grew vines on trellises, and fig-trees, and peach-trees, and cherry-trees. The cherry-trees and peach-trees were in blossom,—lovely showers of white and deep rose-colour among the trembling delicacy of the olives; the fig-leaves were just big enough to smell of figs, the vine-buds were only beginning to show. And beneath these trees were groups of blue and purple irises, and bushes of lavender, and grey, sharp cactuses, and the grass was thick with dandelions and daisies, and right down at the bottom was the sea. Colour seemed flung down anyhow, anywhere; every sort of colour, piled up in heaps, pouring along in rivers—the periwinkles looked exactly as if they were being poured down each side of the steps—and flowers that grow only in borders in England, proud flowers keeping themselves to themselves over there, such as the great blue irises and the lavender, were being jostled by small, shining common things like dandelions

and daisies and the white bells of the wild onion, and only seemed the better and the more exuberant for it.

They stood looking at this crowd of loveliness, this happy jumble, in silence. No, it didn't matter what Mrs. Fisher did; not here; not in such beauty. Mrs. Arbuthnot's discomposure melted out of her. In the warmth and light of what she was looking at, of what to her was a manifestation, an entirely new side, of God, how could one be discomposed? If only Frederick were with her, seeing it too, seeing as he would have seen it when first they were lovers, in the days when he saw what she saw and loved what she loved . . .

She sighed.

"You mustn't sigh in heaven," said Mrs. Wilkins. "One doesn't."

. . . The hot smell from the pine-needles and from the cushions of wild thyme that padded the spaces between the rocks, and sometimes a smell of pure honey from a clump of warm irises up behind them in the sun, puffed across their faces. Very soon Mrs. Wilkinson took her shoes and stockings off, and let her feet hang in the water. After watching her a minute Mrs. Arbuthnot did the same. Their happiness was then complete. Their husbands would not have known them. They left off talking. They ceased to mention heaven. They were just cups of acceptance.

Gardens of LOVE

SONG OF SOLOMON

The Bible

A GARDEN INCLOSED *is* my sister, *my* spouse; a spring shut up, a fountain sealed.

Thy plants *are* an orchard of pomegranates, with pleasant fruits; camphire, with spikenard, spikenard and saffron; calamus and cinnamon, with all trees of frankincense; myrrh and aloes, with all the chief spices: A fountain of gardens, a well of living waters, and streams from Lebanon.

Awake, O north wind; and come, thou south; blow upon my garden, *that* the spices thereof may flow out. Let my beloved come into his garden, and eat his pleasant fruits.

I am come into my garden, my sister, *my* spouse: I have gathered my myrrh with my spice; I have eaten my honeycomb with my honey; I have drunk my wine with my milk: eat, O friends; drink, yea, drink abundantly, O beloved.

The Song of Solomon 4:12–16, 5:1

GIRL GARDENING

Pablo Neruda

YES: I KNEW that your hands were
a blossoming clove and the silvery
lily:
Your notable way
with a furrow
and the flowering marl;
but
when
I saw you delve deeper, dig under
to uncouple the cobble
and limber the roots,
I knew in a moment,
little husbandman,
your heartbeats
were earthen
no less
than your hands;
that there,
you were
shaping
a thing that was always

your own,
touching
the drench
of those doorways
through
which
whirl
the seeds.

So,
plant after plant,
each
fresh
from the planting,
your face
stained
with the kiss
of the ooze,
your flowering
went out
and returned,
you went out
and the tube
of the Alstroemeria
there under your hands
raised its lonely and delicate
presence, the jasmine
devised
a cloud for your temples
starry with scent and the dew.

The whole
of you prospered,
piercing down
into earth,
greening
the light

like a thunderclap
in a massing of leafage and power.
You confided
your seedlings,
my darling,
little red husbandman;
your hand
fondled
the earth
and straightway
the growing was luminous.

Even so,
your watery
fingers,
the dust of your heart,
bring us word
of fecundity, love,
and summon the strength of my songs.
Touching
my heart
while I sleep
trees bloom
on my dream.
I waken and widen my eyes,
and you plant
in my flesh
the darkening stars
that rise
in my song.

So it is, little husbandman:
our loves
are
terrestrial:
your mouth is a planting of lights, a corolla,
and my heart works below in the roots.

THEIR EYES
WERE WATCHING GOD

Zora Neale Hurston

IT WAS A SPRING afternoon in West Florida. Janie had spent most of the day under a blossoming pear tree in the back-yard. She had been spending every minute that she could steal from her chores under that tree for the last three days. That was to say, ever since the first tiny bloom had opened. It had called her to come and gaze on a mystery. From barren brown stems to glistening leaf-buds; from the leaf-buds to snowy virginity of bloom. It stirred her tremendously. How? Why? It was like a flute song forgotten in another existence and remembered again. What? How? Why? This singing she heard that had nothing to do with her ears. The rose of the world was breathing out smell. It followed her through all her waking moments and caressed her in her sleep. It connected itself with other vaguely felt matters that had struck her outside observation and buried themselves in her flesh. Now they emerged and quested about her consciousness.

She was stretched on her back beneath the pear tree soaking in the alto chant of the visiting bees, the gold of the sun and the panting breath of the breeze when the inaudible voice of it all came to her. She saw a dust-bearing bee sink into the sanctum of a bloom; the thousand sister-calyxes arch to meet the love embrace and the ecstatic shiver of the tree from root to tiniest branch creaming in every blossom and frothing with delight. So this was a marriage! She had been summoned to behold a revelation. Then Janie felt a pain remorseless sweet that left her limp and languid.

After a while she got up from where she was and went over the little garden field entire. She was seeking confirmation of the voice and vision, and everywhere she found and acknowledged answers. A personal answer for all other creations except herself. She felt an answer seeking her, but where? When? How? She found herself at the kitchen door and stumbled inside. In the air of the room were flies tumbling and singing, marrying and giving in marriage. When she reached the narrow hallway she was reminded that her grandmother was home with a sick headache. She was lying across the bed asleep so Janie tipped on out of the front door. Oh to be a pear tree—*any* tree in bloom! With kissing bees singing of the beginning of the world! She was sixteen. She had glossy leaves and bursting buds and she wanted to struggle with life but it seemed to elude her. Where were the singing bees for her? Nothing on the place nor in her grandma's house answered her. She searched as much of the world as she could from the top of the front steps and then went on down to the front gate and leaned over to gaze up and down the road. Looking, waiting, breathing short with impatience. Waiting for the world to be made.

THE BARON IN THE TREES

Italo Calvino

COSIMO WAS UP on the holm-oak. The branches spread out, high bridges over the earth. A slight breeze blew; the sun shone. It shone among the leaves so that we had to shade our eyes with our hands to see Cosimo. From the tree Cosimo looked at the world; everything, seen from up there, was different, which was fun in itself. The alley took on a new aspect, and so did the flower-beds, the hortensias, the camellias, the iron table for coffee in the garden. Farther away the tops of the trees thinned out and the kitchen garden merged into little terraced fields, propped by stone walls; the middle distance was dark with olive trees, and beyond that the village of Ombrosa thrust up roofs of slate and faded brick, and down on the port showed the tops of battlements. In the background was the sea, with a high horizon, on which a boat was slowly sailing.

And now out into the garden, after their coffee, came the Baron and the Generalessa. They stood looking at a rose-bush, pretending not to take any notice of Cosimo. They were arm-in-arm first, then soon drew apart to discuss and gesture. But I moved under the holm-oak as if I were playing on my own, though really to try and attract Cosimo's attention; he was still feeling resentful about me, and stayed up there looking away into the distance. I stopped and crouched down under a bench so as to go on watching him without being seen.

My brother sat there like a sentinel. He looked at everything, and everything looked at him. A woman with a basket was passing between the lemon trees. Up the path came a muleteer holding the mane of his mule. The two never set eyes on each

other; at the sound of the metal-shod hoofs the woman turned round and moved towards the path but did not reach it in time. She broke into song then, but the muleteer had already passed the turn; he listened, cracked his whip and said "Aaah!" to the mule; nothing more. Cosimo saw it all.

Now along the path passed the Abbé Fauchelefleur with his open breviary. Cosimo took something from the branch and dropped it on his head; he was not sure what it was, a little spider perhaps, or a piece of bark; anyway, it did not hit him. Cosimo then began to search about with his rapier in a hole of the trunk. Out came a furious bee, he chased it away with a wave of his tricorne and followed its flight with his eyes until it settled on a pumpkin plant. From the house, speedy as ever, came the Cavalier, hurried down the steps into the gardens and vanished among the rows of vines; Cosimo climbed on to a higher branch to see where he went. There was a flutter of wings among the leaves, and out flew a blackbird. Cosimo was rather sorry it had been up there all that time without his noticing it. He looked against the sun for others. No, there were none.

The holm-oak was near an elm: their two crests almost touched. A branch of the elm passed a foot or so above a branch of the other tree; it was easy for my brother to pass and so reach the top of the elm, which we had never explored as it had a high trunk with no branches reachable from the ground. From the elm, by a branch elbow-to-elbow with the next tree, he passed on to a carob, and then to a mulberry tree. So I saw Cosimo swing from one branch to another, high above the garden.

Some branches of the big mulberry tree reached and overlapped the boundary wall of our property, beyond which lay the gardens of the Ondarivas. Although neighbours, we knew none of the Ondariva family, Marquises and Nobles of Ombrosa, as for a number of generations they had enjoyed certain feudal rights claimed by our father, and the two families were separated by mutual antipathy, just as our properties were separated by a high fortress-like wall, put up by either our father or the Marquis, I am not sure which. To this should be added the jealous care which the Ondarivas took of their garden, full, it was said, of the rarest plants. In fact, the grandfather of the present Marquis had been a pupil of the botanist Linnaeus, and since his time all the family connections at the Courts of France and England had been set in motion to send the finest botanical rarities from the colonies; for years boats had landed at the port of Ombrosa sacks of seeds, bundles of cuttings, potted shrubs and even entire trees with huge wrappings of sacking round the roots; until the garden—it was said—had become a mixture of the forests of India and the Americas, and even of New Holland.

All that we were able to see were some dark leaves, growing over the garden wall, of a newly imported tree from the American colonies, the magnolia, from whose black branches sprang a pulpy white flower. Cosimo, on our mulberry, reached the corner of the wall, balanced on it for a moment or two and then, holding on by his hands, jumped on to the other side, amid the flowers and leaves of the magnolia. Then he vanished from sight; and what I am about to tell, as also much else in this account of his life, he described to me afterwards, or I have put together from a few scattered hints and guesses.

Cosimo was on the magnolia. Although the branches were very close together, this was an easy tree to manoeuvre on for a boy so expert in all trees as my brother; and the branches held his weight, although they were slender and of soft wood, so that the points of his shoes tore white wounds of the black bark; he was enveloped in the fresh scent of leaves, turned this way and that by the wind in pages of contrasting greens, dull one moment and glittering the next.

But the whole garden was scented, and although Cosimo could not yet see it clearly, because of all the thick trees, he was already exploring it by smell, and trying to discern the source of the various aromas which he already knew from their being wafted over into our garden by the wind: and these seemed an integral part of the mystery of the place. Then he looked at the branches and saw new leaves, some big and shining as if running water were constantly flowing over them, some tiny and feathered, and tree-trunks either all smooth or all scaly.

There was a great silence. A flight of little wrens went up, chirping. And now a faint voice could be heard singing: "*O la-la . . . O la ba-la-nçoire . . .*" Cosimo looked down. From the branch of a big tree nearby was dangling a swing, and on it was sitting a little girl of about ten years old.

She was a blonde little girl, with hair combed high in an odd style for a child, and a green dress which was also too grown up; its skirt, as it rose with the swing, was swirling with petticoats. The girl had her eyes half closed and her nose in the air as if used to giving orders, and she was eating an apple in little bites, bending her head down towards her hand, which had to hold the apple and balance her on the rope of the swing at the same time; and every time the swing reached the lowest point of its flight she would give herself little pushes on the ground with the end of her tiny shoes, blow out bits of apple peel and sing "*O la-la-la . . . O la ba-la-nçoire . . .*" as if she cared neither for the swing, nor the song, nor (though perhaps a little more) for the apple, and had other thoughts on her mind.

Cosimo dropped from the top of the magnolia to the lower perch, and now had his feet set on each side of a fork and his elbows leaning on a branch in front like a window-sill. The flight of the swing was bringing the little girl right up under his nose.

She was not watching and did not notice. Then suddenly she saw him there, standing on the tree, in tricorne and gaiters. "Oh!" she said.

The apple fell from her hand and rolled away to the foot of the magnolia. Cosimo drew his rapier, leant down from the lowest branch, skewered the apple and offered it to the girl, who had meanwhile made a complete turn on the swing and was up there again. "Take it, it's not dirty, only a little bruised on one side."

The fair little girl now seemed to be regretting she had shown so much surprise at the sudden appearance of this unknown boy on the magnolia, and put on her disdainful air again with her nose in the air. "Are you a thief?" she said.

"A thief?" exclaimed Cosimo, offended; then he thought it over; the idea rather pleased him. "Yes I am," he said, doffing his tricorne at her. "Any objection?"

"And what have you come to steal?"

Cosimo looked at the apple which he had skewered on the point of his rapier, and suddenly realised he was hungry, as he had scarcely touched a thing at table. "This apple," said he, and began to peel it with one side of the rapier, which, in spite of family orders, he kept very sharp.

"Then you're a fruit thief," said the girl.

My brother thought of the rabble of poor urchins from Ombrosa, who scrambled over walls and hedges sacking orchards, boys he had been taught to despise and avoid; and for the first time he thought how free and enviable their life must be. Well now: he might become like them, and live as they did, from now on. "Yes," he said. He cut the apple into slices and began eating it.

The fair girl broke into a laugh which lasted a whole flight of the swing up and down. "Oh, go on! The boys who steal fruit! I know them all! They're all friends of mine! And they go round barefoot, in shirt sleeves and tousled hair, not gaiters and powder!"

My brother went as red as the apple peel. To be laughed at not only for his powdered hair, which he didn't like at all, but also for his gaiters, which he liked a lot, to be considered inferior in appearance to a fruit thief, to boys he had despised till a moment before, and above all to find that this girl who seemed quite at home in the Ondariva gardens was a friend of all the fruit thieves but not of his, all this made him feel annoyed, jealous and ashamed.

"O la-la-la . . . In gaiters and powder!" hummed the little girl on the swing.

For a moment his pride was stung. "I'm not a thief like the boys you know!" he shouted. "I'm not a thief at all! I only said that to frighten you; if you really knew who I was you'd die of fright! I'm a brigand, a terrible brigand!"

The little girl went on flying through the air under his nose, almost as if wanting to graze him with the point of her shoes. "Oh, nonsense. Where's your musket? Brigands all have muskets! And catapaults! I've seen them! They've stopped our coach five times on the way here from the castle!"

"But not the chief! I'm the chief! The chief of the brigands doesn't carry a musket! Only a sword!" and he held out his little rapier.

The little girl shrugged her shoulders. "The chief brigand," she said, "is a man called Gian dei Brughi, and he always brings me presents at Christmas and Easter!"

"Ah!" exclaimed Cosimo di Rondò, seized by a wave of family rancour, "then my father's right when he says that the Marquis of Ondariva is the protector of all the brigands and smugglers around."

The girl swept down to the ground and instead of giving herself a push, braked with a quick little stamp of the foot, and jumped off. The empty swing leapt back into the air on its ropes. "Get down from there at once! How dare you come on to our land!" she exclaimed, pointing a furious finger at the boy.

"I haven't and I won't come on to it," answered Cosimo with equal warmth, "I've never set foot on your land, and I wouldn't for all the gold in the world!"

Then the girl very calmly took up a fan lying on a wicker chair, and though it was not very hot, began fanning herself and walking up and down. "Now," she said in a steady voice, "I'll call the servants and have you taken and beaten! That'll teach you to trespass on our land!" She was constantly changing tone, this girl, putting my brother out every time.

"Where I am isn't land and isn't yours!" proclaimed Cosimo, and felt tempted to add: "And I'm Duke of Ombrosa too, and lord of the whole area," but he held himself back, as he did not want to repeat things his father was always saying now that he had quarrelled with him and run away from his table; he did not want to and did not think it right; also those claims to the dukedom had always seemed just obsessions to him; why should he, Cosimo, now start boasting of being a duke? But he did not want to distract himself and so went on saying whatever came into his head. "This isn't yours," he repeated, "because it's the ground that's yours, and if I put a foot on it I would be trespassing. But up here, I can go wherever I like."

"Oh, so it's all yours up there . . ."

"Yes! It's all mine up here," and he waved vaguely towards the branches, the leaves against the sun, the sky. "On the branches it's all mine. Tell 'em to come and fetch me, and just see if they can!"

Now, after all that boasting, he half expected her to begin jeering at him in some way. Instead of which she seemed suddenly interested. "Ah yes? And how far does it reach, this property of yours?"

"As far as I can get on the trees, here, there, beyond the wall, in the love groves, up the hill, the other side of the hill, the wood, the Bishop's land . . . "

"As far as France?"

"As far as Poland and Saxony," said Cosimo, who knew nothing of geography but the names he had heard from our mother when she talked of the Wars of Succession. "But I'm not selfish like you. I invite you into my property." Now they were calling each other by the familiar *"tu"*; it was she who had begun.

"And whose is the swing, then?" said she, sitting down and opening her fan.

"The swing's yours," pronounced Cosimo, "but as it's tied to this tree, it depends on me. So, when you're touching the earth with your feet you're in your property, when you're in the air you're in mine."

She gave herself a push and flew off, her hands tight on the ropes. Cosimo jumped from the magnolia on to the thick branch which held the swing, seized the ropes from there and began pushing her himself. The swing went higher and higher.

"Are you frightened?"

"No, not me. What's your name?"

"Mine's Cosimo . . . And yours?"

"Violante but they call me Viola."

"They call me Mino, too, as Cosimo's an old man's name."

"I don't like it."

"Cosimo?"

"No, Mino."

"Ah . . . you can call me Cosimo."

"Wouldn't think of it! Listen, you, we must get things straight."

"How d'you mean?" exclaimed he, who found everything she said disturbed him.

"What I say! I can come up into your property and be an honoured guest, d'you see? I come and go as I please. You, though, are sacred and untouchable while you stay in the trees, on your property, but as soon as you set a foot on the soil of my garden you become my slave and I put you in chains."

"No, I'm not coming down into your garden or into mine either ever again. It's all enemy territory to me. You come up with me, and your friends who steal fruit, and perhaps my brother Biagio too, though he's a bit of a coward, and we'll make an army in the trees and bring the earth and the people on it to their senses."

"No, no, not at all. Just let me explain how things are. You have the lordship of the trees, all right? But if you touch the earth just once with your foot, you lose your whole kingdom and become the humblest slave. D'you understand? Even if a branch breaks under you and you fall, it's the end of you!"

"I've never fallen from a tree in my life!"

"No, of course not, but if you do fall, if you do, you change into ashes and the wind'll carry you away."

"Fairy tales. I'm not coming down to the ground because I don't want to."

"Ah, what a bore you are!"

"No, no, let's play. For instance, can I come on to the swing?"

"Yes, if you manage to sit on it without touching the ground."

Near Viola's swing was another one, hanging on the same branch, but pulled up by a knot in the ropes so it should not bump against the other. Cosimo let himself down from the branch by gripping one of the ropes, an exercise he was very good at as our mother had made him do a lot of gymnastics, reached the knot, undid it, stood up on the swing and to give himself impetus bent down on his knees and rocked the weight of his body to and fro. So he got higher and higher. The two swings moved in opposite directions, at the same height now, and passed each other half-way.

"But if you try sitting down and giving a push with your feet you'll go higher," insinuated Viola.

Cosimo made a face at her.

"Come down and give me a push, now, do," said she, smiling sweetly at him.

"No, I said I wouldn't come down at any cost . . ." And Cosimo began to feel put out again.

"Do, please."

"No."

"Ah, hah! You nearly fell into the trap! If you'd set a foot on the ground you'd have lost everything!" Viola got off her swing and began giving little pushes to Cosimo's. "Oh!" Suddenly she had snatched the seat of the swing on which my brother was standing and overturned it. Luckily Cosimo was holding tight to the ropes. Otherwise he would have dropped to the ground like a sausage.

"Cheat!" he cried, and clambered up again on the two ropes, but going up was much more difficult than coming down, particularly with the fair-haired girl maliciously pulling the ropes as hard as she could.

Finally he reached the big branch, and got astride it. With his lace jabot he wiped the sweat on his forehead. "Ah! Ah! You didn't get me!"

"Very nearly."

"But I thought you were a friend!"

"You thought!" and she began fanning herself again.

"Violante!" broke in a sharp female voice at that moment. "Who are you talking to?"

On the white flight of steps leading to the house had appeared a tall, thin lady, with a very wide skirt; she was looking through a lorgnette. Alarmed, Cosimo drew back into the leaves.

"With a young man, *ma tante*," said the little girl, "who was born on the top of a tree and is under a spell so he can't set foot on the ground."

Cosimo, scarlet in the face, asked himself if the little girl was talking like that to make fun of him in front of her aunt, or to make fun of the aunt in front of him, or just to continue the game, or because she did not care a rap about either him or the aunt or the game and he saw he was being watched through the lorgnette, whose owner had approached the tree and was gazing at him as if he was some strange parrot.

"Uh, mais c'est un des Piovasques, ce jeune homme, je crois. Viens, Violante."

Cosimo bridled with shame; the way the aunt recognised him so easily without even asking herself why he was there and at once called the girl away firmly though not severely, the way Viola followed her aunt's call docilely without even turning round, it all suggested that they considered him of no importance, a person who scarcely existed. And so that extraordinary afternoon of his looked like fading into a cloud of self-pity.

Then suddenly the girl made a sign to her aunt, the aunt lowered her head, and the child whispered in her ear. The aunt pointed her lorgnette at Cosimo again. "Well, young man," she said, "would you care to take a dish of chocolate with us? Then we too can get to know you," and here she gave a sideways glance at Viola, "as you're already a friend of the family."

Cosimo sat there staring round-eyed at aunt and niece. His heart was beating fast. Here he was being invited by the Ondarivas of Ombrosa, the most powerful family in the neighbourhood, and the humiliation of a moment before changed to triumph: he was getting his own back on his father by this invitation from the enemies who had always snubbed them, and Viola had interceded for him, and he was now officially accepted as a friend of hers and would play with her in that garden so different from all other gardens. All this Cosimo felt, but an opposite, though confused emotion at the same time; an emotion made up of shyness, pride, loneliness and punctilio; and amid this contrast of feelings my brother seized the branch above him, climbed it, moved into the leafiest part, on to another tree, and vanished.

THE MOWER
TO THE GLOWWORMS

Andrew Marvell

YE LIVING LAMPS, by whose dear light
The nightingale does sit so late,
And studying all the summer night,
Her matchless songs does meditate;

Ye country comets, that portend
No war, nor prince's funeral,
Shining unto no higher end
Than to presage the grass's fall;

Ye glowworms, whose officious flame
To wandering mowers shows the way,
That in the night have lost their aim,
And after foolish fires do stray;

Your courteous lights in vain you waste,
Since Juliana here is come,
For she my mind hath so displaced
That I shall never find my home.

Gardens of TEMPTATION

FROM *PARADISE LOST*
THE TEMPTATION OF EVE

John Milton

...EVE SEPARATE he spies,
Veiled in a cloud of fragrance, where she stood,
Half spied, so thick the roses bushing round
About her glowed, oft stooping to support
Each flower of slender stalk, whose head though gay
Carnation, purple, azure, or specked with gold,
Hung drooping unsustained, them she upstays
Gently with myrtle band, mindless the while,
Her self, though fairest unsupported flower,
From her best prop so far, and storm so nigh.
Nearer he drew, and many a walk traversed
Of stateliest covert, cedar, pine, or palm,
Then voluble and bold, now hid, now seen
Among thick-woven arborets and flowers
Embordered on each bank, the hand of Eve:
Spot more delicious than those gardens feigned
Or of revived Adonis, or renowned
Alcinous, host of old Laertes' son,
Or that, not mystic, where the sapient king

Held dalliance with his fair Egyptian spouse.
Much he the place admired, the person more.
As one who long in populous city pent,
Where houses thick and sewers annoy the air,
Forth issuing on a summer's morn to breathe
Among the pleasant villages and farms
Adjoined, from each thing met conceives delight,
The smell of grain, or tedded grass, or kine,
Or dairy, each rural sight, each rural sound;
If chance with nymph-like step fair virgin pass,
What pleasing seemed, for her now pleases more,
She most, and in her look sums all delight.
Such pleasure took the serpent to behold
This flowery plat, the sweet recess of Eve
Thus early, thus alone; her heavenly form
Angelic, but more soft, and feminine,
Her graceful innocence, her every air
Of gesture or least action overawed
His malice, and with rapine sweet bereaved
His fierceness of the fierce intent it brought:
That space the evil one abstracted stood
From his own evil, and for the time remained
Stupidly good, of enmity disarmed,
Of guile, of hate, of envy, of revenge;
But the hot hell that always in him burns,
Though in mid heaven, soon ended his delight,
And tortures him now more, the more he sees
Of pleasure not for him ordained: then soon
Fierce hate, he recollects, and all his thoughts
Of mischief, gratulating, thus excites.

. . . toward Eve
Addressed his way, not with indented wave,
Prone on the ground, as since, but on his rear,
Circular base of rising folds, that towered

Fold above fold a surging maze, his head
Crested aloft, and carbuncle his eyes;
With burnished neck of verdant gold, erect
Amidst his circling spires, that on the grass
Floated redundant: pleasing was his shape,
And lovely, never since of serpent kind
Lovelier . . .
. . . With tract oblique
At first, as one who sought access, but feared
To interrupt, sidelong he works his way.
. . . Oft he bowed
His turret crest, and sleek enamelled neck,
Fawning, and licked the ground whereon she trod.
His gentle dumb expression turned at length
The eye of Eve to mark his play; he glad
Of her attention gained, with serpent tongue
Organic, or impulse of vocal air,
His fraudulent temptation thus began.
. . . Empress of this fair world, resplendent Eve,
Easy to me it is to tell thee all
What thou command'st, and right thou shouldst be
    obeyed:
I was at first as other beasts that graze
The trodden herb, of abject thoughts and low,
As was my food, nor aught but food discerned
Or sex, and apprehended nothing high:
Till on a day roving the field, I chanced
A goodly tree far distant to behold
Loaden with fruit of fairest colours mixed,
Ruddy and gold: I nearer drew to gaze;
When from the boughs a savoury odour blown,
Grateful to appetite, more pleased my sense
Than smell of sweetest fennel or the teats
Of ewe or goat dropping the milk at even,

Unsucked of lamb or kid, that tend their play.
To satisfy the sharp desire I had
Of tasting those fair apples, I resolved
Not to defer; hunger and thirst at once,
Powerful persuaders, quickened at the scent
Of that alluring fruit, urged me so keen.
About the mossy trunk I wound me soon,
For high from ground the branches would require
Thy utmost reach or Adam's: round the tree
All other beasts that saw, with like desire
Longing and envying stood, but could not reach.
Amid the tree now got, where plenty hung
Tempting so nigh, to pluck and eat my fill
I spared not, for such pleasure till that hour
At feed or fountain never had I found.
Sated at length, ere long I might perceive
Strange alteration in me, to degree
Of reason in my inward powers, and speech
Wanted not long, though to this shape retained.
Thenceforth to speculations high or deep
I turned my thoughts, and with capacious mind
Considered all things visible in heaven,
Or earth, or middle, all things fair and good;
But all that fair and good in thy divine
Semblance, and in thy beauty's heavenly ray
United I beheld; no fair to thine
Equivalent or second, which compelled
me thus, though importune perhaps, to come
And gaze, and worship thee of right declared
Sovereign of creatures, universal dame.
    So talked the spirited sly snake; and Eve
Yet more amazed unwary thus replied.
    Serpent, thy overpraising leaves in doubt
The virtue of that fruit, in thee first proved:

But say, where grows the tree, from hence how far?
For many are the trees of God that grow
In Paradise, and various, yet unknown
To us, in such abundance lies our choice,
As leaves a greater store of fruit untouched,
Still hanging incorruptible, till men
Grow up to their provision, and more hands
Help to disburden nature of her birth.

    To whom the wily adder: blithe and glad.
Empress, the way is ready, and not long,
Beyond a row of myrtles, on a flat,
Fast by a fountain, one small thicket past
Of blowing myrrh and balm; if thou accept
My conduct, I can bring thee thither soon.

    Lead then, said Eve. He leading swiftly rolled
In tangles, and made intricate seem straight,
To mischief swift. Hope elevates, and joy
Brightens his crest, as when a wandering fire,
Compact of unctuous vapour, which the night
Condenses, and the cold environs round,
Kindles through agitation to a flame,
Which oft, they say, some evil spirit attends
Hovering and blazing with delusive light,
Misleads the amazed night-wanderer from his way
To bogs and mires, and oft through pond or pool,
There swallowed up and lost, from succour far.
So glistered the dire snake, and into fraud
Led Eve our credulous mother, to the tree
Of prohibition, root of all our woe;
Which when she saw, thus to her guide she spake.

    Serpent, we might have spared our coming hither,
Fruitless to me, though fruit be here to excess,
The credit of whose virtue rest with thee,
Wondrous indeed, if cause of such effects.

But of this tree we may not taste nor touch;
God so commanded, and left that command
Sole daughter of his voice; the rest, we live
Law to our selves, our reason is our law.
    To whom the tempter guilefully replied.
Indeed? Hath God then said that of the fruit
Of all these garden trees ye shall not eat,
Yet lords declared of all in earth or air?
    To whom thus Eve yet sinless. Of the fruit
Of each tree in the garden we may eat,
But of the fruit of this fair tree amidst
The garden, God hath said, Ye shall not eat
Thereof, nor shall ye touch it, lest ye die.
    She scarce had said, though brief, when now
        more bold

The tempter, but with show of zeal and love
To man, and indignation at his wrong,
New parts puts on, and as to passion moved,
Fluctuates disturbed, yet comely and in act
raised, as of some great matter to begin.
As when of old some orator renowned
In Athens or free Rome, where eloquence
Flourished, since mute, to some great cause addressed,
Stood in himself collected, while each part,
Motion, each act won audience ere the tongue,
Sometimes in highth began, as no delay
Of preface brooking through his zeal of right.
So standing, moving, or to highth upgrown
The tempter all impassioned thus began.
    O sacred, wise, and wisdom-giving plant,
Mother of science, now I feel thy power
Within me clear, not only to discern
Things in their causes, but to trace the ways
Of highest agents, deemed however wise.

Queen of this universe, do not believe
Those rigid threats of death; ye shall not die:
How should ye? By the fruit? It gives you life
To knowledge. By the threatener? Look on me,
Me who have touched and tasted, yet both live,
And life more perfect have attained than fate
Meant me, by venturing higher than my lot.
Shall that be shut to man, which to the beast
Is open? Or will God incense his ire
For such a petty trespass, and not praise
Rather your dauntless virtue, whom the pain
Of death denounced, whatever thing death be,
Deterred, not from achieving what might lead
To happier life, knowledge of good and evil;
Of good, how just? Of evil, if what is evil
Be real, why not known, since easier shunned?
God therefore cannot hurt ye, and be just;
Not just, not God; not feared then, nor obeyed:
Your fear itself of death removes the fear.
Why then was this forbid? Why but to awe,
Why but to keep ye low and ignorant,
His worshippers; he knows that in the day
Ye eat thereof, your eyes that seem so clear,
Yet are but dim, shall perfectly be then
Opened and cleared, and ye shall be as gods,
Knowing both good and evil as they know.
That ye should be as gods, since I as man,
Internal man, is but proportion meet,
I of brute human, ye of human gods.
So ye shall die perhaps, by putting off
Human, to put on gods, death to be wished,
Though threatened, which no worse than this can
    bring.
And what are gods that man may not become

As they, participating godlike food?
The gods are first, and that advantage use
On our belief, that all from them proceeds;
I question it, for this fair earth I see,
Warmed by the sun, producing every kind,
Them nothing: if they all things, who enclosed
Knowledge of good and evil in this tree,
That whoso eats thereof, forthwith attains
Wisdom without their leave? And wherein lies
The offence, that man should thus attain to know?
What can your knowledge hurt him, or this tree
Impart against his will if all be his?
Or is it envy, and can envy dwell
In heavenly breasts? These, these and many more
Causes import your need of this fair fruit.
Goddess humane, reach then, and freely taste.
      He ended, and his words replete with guile
Into her heart too easy entrance won:
Fixed on the fruit she gazed, which to behold
Might tempt alone, and in her ears the sound
Yet rung of his persuasive words, impregned
With reason, to her seeming, and with truth;
Mean while the hour of noon drew on, and waked
An eager appetite, raised by the smell
So savoury of that fruit, which with desire,
Inclinable now grown to touch or taste,
Solicited her longing eye; yet first
Pausing a while, thus to her self she mused.
. . . If death
Bind us with after-bands, what profits then
Our inward freedom? In the day we eat
Of this fair fruit, our doom is, we shall die.
How dies the serpent? He hath eaten and lives,
And knows, and speaks, and reasons, and discerns,
Irrational till then. For us alone

Was death invented? Or to us denied
This intellectual food, for beasts reserved?
For beasts it seems: yet that one beast which first
Hath tasted, envies not, but brings with joy
The good befallen him, author unsuspect,
Friendly to man, far from deceit or guile.
What fear I then, rather what know to fear
Under this ignorance of good and evil,
Of God or death, of law or penalty?
Here grows the cure of all, this fruit divine,
Fair to the eye, inviting to the taste,
Of virtue to make wise: what hinders then
To reach, and feed at once both body and mind?
    So saying, her rash hand in evil hour
Forth reaching to the fruit, she plucked, she ate:
Earth felt the wound, and nature from her seat
Sighing through all her works gave signs of woe,
That all was lost. Back to the thicket slunk
The guilty serpent, and well might, for Eve
Intent now wholly on her taste, naught else
Regarded, such delight till then, as seemed,
In fruit she never tasted, whether true
Or fancied so, through expectation high
Of knowledge, nor was godhead from her thought.
Greedily she engorged without restraint,
And knew not eating death.

RAPPACCINI'S DAUGHTER

Nathaniel Hawthorne

A YOUNG MAN, named Giovanni Guasconti, came, very long ago, from the more southern region of Italy, to pursue his studies at the University of Padua. Giovanni, who had but a scanty supply of gold ducats in his pocket, took lodgings in a high and gloomy chamber of an old edifice which looked not unworthy to have been the palace of a Paduan noble, and which, in fact exhibited over its entrance the armorial bearings of a family long since extinct. The young stranger, who was not unstudied in the great poem of his country recollected that one of the ancestors of this family, and perhaps an occupant of this very mansion, had been pictured by Dante as a partaker of the immortal agonies of his Inferno. These reminiscences and associations, together with the tendency to heartbreak natural to a young man for the first time out of his native sphere, caused Giovanni to sigh heavily as he looked around the desolate and ill-furnished apartment.

"Holy Virgin, signor!" cried the old Dame Lisabetta, who, won by the youth's remarkable beauty of person was kindly endeavouring to give the chamber a habitable air, "what a sigh was that to come out of a young man's heart! Do you find this old mansion gloomy? For the love of Heaven, then, put your head out of the window, and you will see as bright sunshine as you have left in Naples."

Guasconti mechanically did as the old woman advised, but could not quite agree with her that the Paduan sunshine was as cheerful as that of southern Italy. Such as it was, however, it fell upon a garden beneath the window and expended its fostering influences on a variety of plants, which seemed to have been cultivated with exceeding care.

"Does this garden belong to the house?" asked Giovanni.

"Heaven forbid, signor, unless it were fruitful of better pot herbs than any that grow there now," answered old Lisabetta. "No; that garden is cultivated by the own hands of Signor Giacomo Rappaccini, the famous doctor, who, I warrant him, has been heard of as far as Naples. It is said that he distils these plants into medicines that are as potent as a charm. Oftentimes you may see the signor doctor at work, and perchance the signora, his daughter, too, gathering the strange flowers that grow in the garden."

The old woman had now done what she could for the aspect of the chamber; and, commending the young man to the protection of the saints, took her departure.

Giovanni still found no better occupation than to look down into the garden beneath his window. From its appearance, he judged it to be one of those botanic gardens which were of earlier date in Padua than elsewhere in Italy or in the world. Or, not improbably, it might once have been the pleasure-place of an opulent family; for there was the ruin of a marble fountain in the centre, sculptured with rare art, but so woefully shattered that it was impossible to trace the original design from the chaos of remaining fragments. The water, however, continued to gush and sparkle into the sunbeams as cheerfully as ever. A little gurgling sound ascended to the young man's window, and made him feel as if the fountain were an immortal spirit that sung its song unceasingly and without heeding the vicissitudes around it, while one century imbedded it in marble and another scattered the perishable garniture on the soil. All about the pool into which the water subsided grew various plants, that seemed to require a plentiful supply of moisture for the nourishment of gigantic leaves, and, in some instances, flowers gorgeously magnificent. There was one shrub in particular, set in a marble vase in the midst of the pool, that bore a profusion of purple blossoms, each of which had the lustre and richness of a gem; and the whole together made a show so resplendent that it seemed enough to illuminate the garden, even had there been no sunshine. Every portion of the soil was peopled with plants and herbs, which, if less beautiful, still bore tokens of assiduous care, as if all had their individual virtues, known to the scientific mind that fostered them. Some were placed in urns, rich with old carving, and others in common garden pots; some crept serpent-like along the ground or climbed on high, using whatever means of ascent was offered them. One plant had wreathed itself round a statue of Vertumnus, which was thus quite veiled and shrouded in a drapery of hanging foliage, so happily arranged that it might have served a sculptor for a study.

While Giovanni stood at the window he heard a rustling behind a screen of leaves, and became aware that a person was at work in the garden. His figure soon emerged into view, and showed itself to be that of no common laborer, but a tall, emaciated, sallow, and sickly-looking man, dressed in a scholar's garb of black. He was beyond the middle term of life, with gray hair, a thin, gray beard, and a face singularly marked with intellect and cultivation, but which could never, even in his more youthful days, have expressed much warmth of heart.

Nothing could exceed the intentness with which this scientific gardener examined every shrub which grew in his path: it seemed as if he was looking into their inmost nature, making observations in regard to their creative essence, and discovering why one leaf grew in this shape and another in that, and wherefore such and such flowers differed among themselves in hue and perfume. Nevertheless, in spite of this deep intelligence on his part, there was no approach to intimacy between himself and these vegetable existences. On the contrary, he avoided their actual touch or the direct inhaling of their odors with a caution that impressed Giovanni most disagreeably; for the man's demeanor was that of one walking among malignant influences, such as savage beasts, or deadly snakes, or evil spirits, which, should he allow them one moment of license, would wreak upon him some terrible fatality. It was strangely frightful to the young man's imagination to see this air of insecurity in a person cultivating a garden, that most simple and innocent of human toils, and which had been alike the joy and labor of the unfallen parents of the race. Was this garden, then, the Eden of the present world? And this man, with such a perception of harm in what his own hands caused to grow—was he Adam?

The distrustful gardener, while plucking away the dead leaves or pruning the too luxuriant growth of the shrubs, defended his hands with a pair of thick gloves. Nor were these his only armor. When, in his walk through the garden, he came to the magnificent plant that hung its purple gems beside the marble fountain, he placed a kind of mask over his mouth and nostrils, as if all this beauty did but conceal a deadlier malice; but, finding his task still too dangerous, he drew back, removed the mask, and called loudly, but in the infirm voice of a person affected with inward disease,—

"Beatrice! Beatrice!"

"Here am I, my father. What would you?" cried a rich and youthful voice from the window of the opposite house—a voice as rich as a tropical sunset, and which made Giovanni, thought he knew not why, think of deep hues of purple or crimson and of perfumes heavily delectable. "Are you in the garden?"

"Yes, Beatrice," answered the gardener, "and I need your help."

Soon there emerged from under a sculptured portal the figure of a young girl,

arrayed with as much richness of taste as the most splendid of the flowers, beautiful as the day, and with a bloom so deep and vivid that one shade more would have been too much. She looked redundant with life, health, and energy; all of which attributes were bound down and compressed, as it were, and girdled tensely, in their luxuriance, by her virgin zone. Yet Giovanni's fancy must have grown morbid while he looked down into the garden; for the impression which the fair stranger made upon him was as if here were another flower, the human sister of those vegetable ones, as beautiful as they, more beautiful than the richest of them, but still to be touched only with a glove, nor to be approached without a mask. As Beatrice came down the garden path, it was observable that she handled and inhaled the odor of several of the plants which her father had most sedulously avoided.

"Here, Beatrice," said the latter, "see how many needful offices require to be done to our chief treasure. Yet, shattered as I am, my life might pay the penalty of approaching it so closely as circumstances demand. Henceforth, I fear, this plant must be consigned to your sole charge."

"And gladly will I undertake it," cried again the rich tones of the young lady, as she bent towards the magnificent plant and opened her arms as if to embrace it. "Yes, my sister, my splendor, it shall be Beatrice's task to nurse and serve thee; and thou shalt reward her with thy kisses and perfumed breath, which to her is as the breath of life."

Then, with all the tenderness in her manner that was so strikingly expressed in her words, she busied herself with such attentions as the plant seemed to require, and Giovanni, at his lofty window, rubbed his eyes and almost doubted whether it were a girl tending her favorite flower, or one sister performing the duties of affection to another. The scene soon terminated. Whether Dr. Rappaccini had finished his labors in the garden, or that his watchful eye had caught the stranger's face, he now took his daughter's arm and retired. Night was already closing in; oppressive exhalations seemed to proceed from the plants and steal upward past the open window; and Giovanni, closing the lattice, went to his couch and dreamed of a rich flower and beautiful girl. Flower and maiden were different, and yet the same, and fraught with some strange peril in either shape.

. . . At first, as we have said, the garden was a solitude. Soon, however,—as Giovanni had half hoped, half feared, would be the case,—a figure appeared beneath the antique sculptured portal, and came down between the rows of plants, inhaling their various perfumes as if she were one of those beings of old classic fable that lived upon sweet odors. On again beholding Beatrice, the young man was even startled to perceive how much her beauty exceeded his recollection of it; so brilliant, so vivid, was its character, that she glowed amid the sunlight, and, as Giovanni whispered to himself, positively illuminated the more shadowy intervals of the garden path. Her face being now more revealed than on the former occasion, he was struck by its expression of simplicity and sweetness—qualities that had not entered into his idea of her character, and which made him ask anew what manner of mortal she might be. Nor did he fail again to observe, or imagine, an analogy between the beautiful shrub and the gorgeous shrub that hung its gemlike flowers over the fountain—a resemblance which Beatrice seemed to have indulged a fantastic humor in heightening, both by the arrangement of her dress and the selection of its hues.

Approaching the shrub, she threw open her arms, as with a passionate ardor, and drew its branches into an intimate embrace—so intimate that her features were hidden in its leafy bosom and her glistening ringlets all intermingled with the flowers.

"Give me thy breath, my sister," exclaimed Beatrice, "for I am faint with common air. And give me this flower of thine, which I separate with gentlest fingers from the stem and place it close beside my heart."

With these words the beautiful daughter of Rappaccini plucked one of the richest blossoms of the shrub, and was about to fasten it in her bosom. But now, unless Giovanni's draughts of wine had bewildered his senses, a singular incident occurred. A small orange-colored reptile, of the lizard or chameleon species, chanced to be creeping along the path, just at the feet of Beatrice. It appeared to Giovanni,—but, at the distance from which he gazed, he could scarcely have seen anything so minute,—it appeared to him, however, that a drop or two of moisture from the broken stem of the flower descended upon the lizard's head. For an instant the reptile contorted itself violently, and then lay motionless in the sunshine. Beatrice observed this remarkable phenomenon, and crossed herself, sadly, but without surprise; nor did she therefore hesitate to arrange that fatal flower in her bosom. There it blushed, and almost glimmered with the dazzling effect of a precious stone, adding to her dress and aspect the one appropriate charm which nothing else in the world could have supplied. But Giovanni, out of the shadow of his window, bent forward and shrank back, and murmured and trembled.

"Am I awake? Have I my senses?" said he to himself. "What is this being? Beautiful shall I call her, or inexpressibly terrible?"

Beatrice now strayed carelessly through the garden, approaching closer beneath Giovanni's window, so that he was compelled to thrust his head quite out of its concealment in order to gratify the intense and painful curiosity which she excited. At this moment there came a beautiful insect over the garden wall: it had, perhaps, wandered through the city, and found no flowers or verdure among those antique haunts of men until the heavy perfumes of Dr. Rappaccini's shrubs had lured it from afar. Without alighting on the flowers, this winged brightness seemed to be attracted by Beatrice, and lingered in the air and fluttered about her head. Now, here it could not be but that Giovanni Guasconti's eyes deceived him. Be that as it might, he fancied that, while Beatrice was gazing at the insect with childish delight, it grew faint and fell at her feet; its bright wings shivered; it was dead—from no cause that he could discern, unless it were the atmosphere of her breath. Again Beatrice crossed herself and sighed heavily as she bent over the dead insect.

An impulsive movement of Giovanni drew her eyes to the window. There she beheld the beautiful head of the young man—rather a Grecian than an Italian head, with fair, regular features, and a glistening of gold among his ringlets—gazing down upon her like a being that hovered in mid air. Scarcely knowing what he did, Giovanni threw down the bouquet which he had hitherto held in his hand.

"Signora," said he, "these are pure and healthful flowers. Wear them for the sake of Giovanni Guasconti."

"Thanks, signor," replied Beatrice, with her rich voice, that came forth as it were like a gush of music, and with a mirthful expression half childish and half womanlike. "I accept your gift, and would fain recompense it with this precious

purple flower, but, if I toss it into the air, it will not reach you. So Signor Guasconti must even content himself with my thanks."

She lifted the bouquet from the ground, and then, as if inwardly ashamed at having stepped aside from her maidenly reserve to respond to a stranger's greeting, passed swiftly homeward through the garden. But, few as the moments were, it seemed to Giovanni, when she was on the point of vanishing beneath the sculptured portal, that his beautiful bouquet was already beginning to wither in her grasp. It was an idle thought; there could be no possibility of distinguishing a faded flower from a fresh one at so great a distance.

For many days after this incident the young man avoided the window that looked into Dr. Rappaccini's garden, as if something ugly and monstrous would have blasted his eyesight had he been betrayed into a glance. He felt conscious of having put himself, to a certain extent, within the influence of an unintelligible power by the communication which he had opened with Beatrice. The wisest course would have been, if his heart were in any real danger, to quit his lodgings and Padua itself at once; the next wiser, to have accustomed himself, as far as possible, to the familiar and day-light view of Beatrice—thus bringing her rigidly and systematically within the limits of ordinary experience. Least of all, while avoiding her sight, ought Giovanni to have remained so near this extraordinary being that the proximity and possibility even of intercourse should give a kind of sustenance and reality to the wild vagaries which his imagination ran riot continually in producing. Guasconti had not a deep heart—or, at all events, its depths were not sounded now; but he had a quick fancy, and an ardent southern temperament, which rose every instant to a higher fever pitch. Whether or no Beatrice possessed those terrible attributes, that fatal breath, the affinity with these so beautiful and deadly flowers which were indicated by what Giovanni had witnessed, she had at least instilled a fierce and subtle poison into his system. It was not love, although her rich beauty was a madness to him; nor horror, even while he fancied her spirit to be imbued with the same baneful essence that seemed to pervade her physical frame; but a wild offspring of both love and horror that had each parent in it, and burned like one and shivered like the other. Giovanni knew not what to dread; still less did he know what to hope; yet hope and dread kept a continual warfare in his breast, alternately vanquishing one another and starting up afresh to renew the contest. Blessed are all simple emotions, be they dark or bright! It is the lurid intermixture of the two that produces the illuminating blaze of the infernal regions.

Sometimes he endeavoured to assuage the fever of his spirit by a rapid walk through the streets of Padua or beyond its gates; his footsteps kept time with the throbbings of his brain, so that the walk was apt to accelerate itself to a race. One day he found himself arrested; his arm was seized by a portly personage, who had turned back on recognizing the young man and expended much breath in overtaking him.

"Signor Giovanni! Stay, my young friend!" cried he. "Have you forgotten me? That might well be the case if I were as much altered as yourself."

It was Baglioni, whom Giovanni had avoided ever since their first meeting, from a doubt that the professor's sagacity would look too deeply into his secrets. Endeavoring to recover himself, he stared forth wildly from his inner world into the outer one and spoke like a man in a dream.

"Yes; I am Giovanni Guasconti. You are Professor Pietro Baglioni. Now let me pass!"

"Not yet, not yet, Signor Guasconti," said the professor, smiling, but at the same time scrutinizing the youth with an earnest glance. "What! did I grow up side by side with your father? And shall his son pass me like a stranger in these old streets of Padua? Stand still, Signor Giovanni, for we must have a word or two before we part."

"Speedily, then, most worshipful professor, speedily," said Giovanni, with feverish impatience. "Does not your worship see that I am in haste?"

Now, while he was speaking there came a man in black along the street, stopping and moving feebly like a person in inferior health. His face was all over spread with a sickly and most sallow hue, but yet so pervaded with an expression of piercing and active intellect that an observer might easily have overlooked the merely physical attributes and have seen only this wonderful energy. As he passed, this person exchanged a cold and distant salutation with Baglioni, but fixed his eyes upon Giovanni with an intentness that seemed to bring out whatever was within him worthy of notice. Nevertheless, there was a peculiar quietness in the look, as if taking merely a speculative, not a human, interest in the young man.

"It is Dr. Rappaccini!" whispered the professor when the stranger had passed. "Had he ever seen your face before?"

"Not that I know," answered Giovanni, starting at the name.

"He *has* seen you! he must have seen you!" said Baglioni hastily. "For some purpose or other, this man of science is making a study of you. I know that look of his! It is the same that coldly illuminates his face as he bends over a bird, a mouse, or a butterfly, which, in pursuance of some experiment, he has killed by the perfume of a flower; a look as deep as nature itself, but without nature's warmth of love. Signor Giovanni, I will stake my life upon it, you are the subject of one of his experiments!"

"Will you make a fool of me?" cried Giovanni, passionately. "That, signor professor, were an untoward experiment."

"Patience! patience!" replied the imperturbable professor. "I tell thee, my poor Giovanni, that Rappaccini has a scientific interest in thee. Thou hast fallen into fearful hands! And the Signora Beatrice,—what part does she act in this mystery?"

But Guasconti, finding Baglioni's pertinacity intolerable, here broke away, and was gone before the professor could again seize his arm. He looked after the young man intently and shook his head.

"This must not be," said Baglioni to himself. "The youth is the son of my old friend, and shall not come to any harm from which the arcana of medical science can preserve him. Besides, it is too insufferable an impertinence in Rappaccini thus to snatch the lad out of my hands, as I may say, and make use of him for his infernal experiments. This daughter of his! It shall be looked to. Perchance, most learned Rappaccini, I may foil you where you little dream of it!"

Meanwhile, Giovanni had pursued a circuitous route, and at length found himself at the door of his lodgings. As he crossed the threshold he was met by old Lisabetta, who smirked and smiled, and was evidently desirous to attract his attention; vainly, however, as the ebullition of his feelings had momentarily subsided into a cold and dull vacuity. He turned his eyes full upon the withered face that was puckering itself into a smile, but seemed to behold it not. The old dame, therefore, laid her grasp upon his cloak.

"Signor! signor!" whispered she, still with a smile over the whole breadth of her visage, so that it looked not unlike a grotesque carving in wood, darkened by centuries. "Listen, signor! There is a private entrance into the garden!"

"What do you say?" exclaimed Giovanni, turning quickly about, as if an inanimate thing should start into feverish life. "A private entrance into Dr. Rappaccini's garden?"

"Hush! hush! not so loud!" whispered Lisabetta, putting her hand over his mouth. "Yes; into the worshipful doctor's garden, where you may see all his fine shrubbery. Many a young man in Padua would give gold to be admitted among those flowers."

Giovanni put a piece of gold into her hand.

"Show me the way," said he.

A surmise, probably excited by his conversation with Baglioni, crossed his mind, that this interposition of old Lisabetta might perchance be connected with the intrigue, whatever were its nature, in which the professor seemed to suppose that Dr. Rappacccini was involving him. But such a suspicion, though it disturbed Giovanni, was inadequate to restrain him. The instant that he was aware of the possibility of approaching Beatrice, it seemed an absolute necessity of his existence to do so. It mattered not whether she were angel or demon; he was irrevocably within her sphere, and must obey the law that whirled him onward, in ever-lessening circles, towards a result which he did not attempt to foreshadow; and yet, strange to say, there came across him a sudden doubt whether this intense interest on his part were not delusory; whether it were really of so deep and positive a nature as to justify him in now thrusting himself into an incalculable position; whether it were not merely the fantasy of a young man's brain, only slightly or not at all connected with his heart.

He paused, hesitated, turned half about, but again went on. His withered guide led him along several obscure passages, and finally undid a door, through which, as it was opened, there came the sight and sound of rustling leaves, with the broken sunshine glimmering among them. Giovanni stepped forth, and forcing himself through the entanglement of a shrub that wreathed its tendrils over the hidden entrance, stood beneath his own window in the open area of Dr. Rappaccini's garden.

How often is it the case that, when impossibilities have come to pass and dreams have condensed their misty substance into tangible realities, we find ourselves calm, and even coldy self-possessed, amid circumstances which it would have been a delirium of joy or agony to anticipate! Fate delights to thwart us thus. Passion will choose his own time to rush upon the scene, and lingers sluggishly behind when an appropriate adjustment of events would seem to summon his appearance. So was it now with Giovanni. Day after day his pulses had throbbed with feverish blood at the improbable idea of an interview with Beatrice, and of standing with her, face to face, in this very garden, basking in the Oriental sunshine of her beauty, and snatching from her full gaze the mystery which he deemed the riddle of his own existence. But now there was a singular and untimely equanimity within his breast. He threw a glance around the garden to discover if Beatrice or her father were present, and, perceiving that he was alone, began a critical observation of the plants.

The aspect of one and all of them dissatisfied him; their gorgeousness seemed fierce, passionate, and even unnatural. There was hardly an individual shrub which a wanderer, straying by himself through a forest, would not have been startled to find growing wild, as if an unearthly face had glared at him out of the thicket. Several also would have shocked a delicate instinct by an appearance of artificialness indicating that there had been such commixture, and, as it were, adultery of various vegetable species, that the production was no longer of God's making, but the monstrous offspring of man's depraved fancy, glowing with only an evil mockery of beauty. They were probably the result of experiment, which in one or two cases had succeeded in mingling plants individually lovely into a compound possessing the questionable and ominous character that distinguished the whole growth of the garden. In fine, Giovanni recognized but two or three plants in the collection, and those of a kind that he well knew to be poisonous. While busy with these contemplations he heard the rustling of a silken garment, and, turning, beheld Beatrice emerging from beneath the sculptured portal.

Giovanni had not considered with himself what should be his deportment; whether he should apologize for his intrusion into the garden, or assume that he was there with the privity at least, if not by the desire, of Dr. Rappaccini or his daughter; but Beatrice's manner placed him at his ease, though leaving him still in doubt by what agency he had gained admittance. She came lightly along the path and met him near the broken fountain. There was surprise in her face, but brightened by a simple and kind expression of pleasure.

"You are a connoisseur in flowers, signor," said Beatrice, with a smile, alluding to the bouquet which he had flung her from the window. "It is no marvel, therefore, if the sight of my father's rare collection has tempted you to take a nearer view. If he were here, he could tell you many strange and interesting facts as to the nature and habits of these shrubs; for he has spent a lifetime in such studies, and this garden is his world."

"And yourself, lady," observed Giovanni, "if fame says true,—you likewise are deeply skilled in the virtues indicated by these rich blossoms and the spicy perfumes. Would you deign to be my instructress, I should prove an apter scholar than if taught by Signor Rappaccini himself."

"Are there such idle rumors?" asked Beatrice, with the music of a pleasant laugh. "Do people say that I am skilled in my father's science of plants? What a jest is there! No; though I have grown up among these flowers, I know no more of them than their hues and perfume; and sometimes methinks I would fain rid myself of even that small knowledge. There are many flowers here, and those not the least brilliant, that shock and offend me when they meet my eye. But pray, signor, do not believe these stories about my science. Believe nothing of me save what you see with your own eyes."

"And must I believe all that I have seen with my own eyes?" asked Giovanni, pointedly, while the recollection of former scenes made him shrink. "No, signora; you demand too little of me. Bid me believe nothing save what comes from your own lips."

It would appear that Beatrice understood him. There came a deep flush to her cheek; but she looked full into Giovanni's eyes, and responded to his gaze of uneasy suspicion with a queenlike haughtiness.

"I do so bid you, signor," she replied. "Forget whatever you may have fancied in regard to me. If true to the outward senses, still it may be false in its essence; but the words of Beatrice Rappaccini's lips are true from the depths of the heart outward. Those you may believe."

A fervor glowed in her whole aspect and beamed upon Giovanni's consciousness like the light of truth itself; but while she spoke there was a fragrance in the atmosphere around her, rich and delightful, though evanescent, yet which the young man, from an indefinable reluctance, scarcely dared to draw into his lungs. It might be the odor of the flowers. Could it be Beatrice's breath which thus embalmed her words with a strange richness, as if by steeping them in her heart? A faintness passed like a shadow over Giovanni and flitted away; he seemed to gaze through the beautiful girl's eyes into her transparent soul, and felt no more doubt or fear.

The tinge of passion that had colored Beatrice's manner vanished; she became gay, and appeared to derive a pure delight from her communion with the youth not unlike what the maiden of a lonely island might have felt conversing with a voyager from the civilized world. Evidently her experience of life had been confined within the limits of that garden. She talked now about matters as simple as the daylight or summer clouds, and now asked questions in reference to the city, or Giovanni's dis-

tant home, his friends, his mother, and his sisters—questions indicating such seclu-
sion, and such a lack of familiarity with modes and forms, that Giovanni responded
as if to an infant. Her spirit gushed out before him like a fresh rill that was just catching its first glimpse of the sunlight and wondering at the reflections of earth and sky
which were flung into its bosom. There came thoughts, too, from a deep source, and
fantasies of a gemlike brilliancy, as if diamonds and rubies sparkled upward among
the bubbles of the fountain. Ever and anon there gleamed across the young man's
mind a sense of wonder that he should be walking side by side with the being who
had so wrought upon his imagination, whom he had idealized in such hues of terror,
in whom he had positively witnessed such manifestations of dreadful attributes—that
he should be conversing with Beatrice like a brother, and should find her so human
and so maidenlike. But such reflections were only momentary; the effect of her character was too real not to make itself familiar at once.

In this free intercourse they had strayed through the garden, and now, after
many turns among its avenues, were come to the shattered fountain, beside which
grew the magnificent shrub, with its treasury of glowing blossoms. A fragrance was
diffused from it which Giovanni recognized as identical with that which he had
attributed to Beatrice's breath, but incomparably more powerful. As her eyes fell
upon it, Giovanni beheld her press her hand to her bosom as if her heart were throb-
bing suddenly and painfully.

"For the first time in my life," murmured she, addressing the shrub, "I had forgotten thee."

"I remember, signora," said Giovanni, "that you once promised to reward me
with one of those living gems for the bouquet which I had the happy boldness to
fling at your feet. Permit me now to pluck it as a memorial of this interview."

He made a step towards the shrub with extended hand; but Beatrice darted forward, uttering a shriek that went through his heart like a dagger. She caught his hand
and drew it back with the whole force of her slender figure. Giovanni felt her touch
thrilling through his fibres.

"Touch it not!" exclaimed she, in a voice of agony. "Not for thy life! It is fatal!"

Then, hiding her face, she fled from him and vanished beneath the sculptured
portal. As Giovanni followed her with his eyes, he beheld the emaciated figure and
pale intelligence of Dr. Rappaccini, who had been watching the scene, he knew not
how long, within the shadow of the entrance.

No sooner was Guasconti alone in his chamber than the image of Beatrice came
back to his passionate musings, invested with all the witchery that had been gathering
around it ever since his first glimpse of her, and now likewise imbued with a tender

warmth of girlish womanhood. She was human; her nature was endowed with all gentle and feminine qualities; she was worthiest to be worshipped; she was capable, surely, on her part, of the height and heroism of love. Those tokens which he had hitherto considered as proofs of a frightful peculiarity in her physical and moral system were now either forgotten or by the subtle sophistry of passion transmitted into a golden crown of enchantment, rendering Beatrice the more admirable by so much as she was the more unique. Whatever had looked ugly was now beautiful; or, if incapable of such a change, it stole away and hid itself among these shapeless half ideas which throng the dim region beyond the daylight of our perfect consciousness. Thus did he spend the night, nor fell asleep until the dawn had begun to awake the slumbering flowers in Dr. Rappaccini's garden, whither Giovanni's dreams doubtless led him. Up rose the sun in his due season, and, flinging his beams upon the young man's eyelids, awoke him to a sense of pain. When thoroughly aroused, he became sensible of a burning and tingling agony in his hand—in his right hand—the very hand which Beatrice had grasped in her own when he was on the point of plucking one of the gemlike flowers. On the back of that hand there was now a purple print like that of four small fingers, and the likeness of a slender thumb upon his wrist.

O, how stubbornly does love,—or even that cunning semblance of love which flourishes in the imagination, but strikes no depth of root into the heart,—how stubbornly does it hold its faith until the moment comes when it is doomed to vanish into thin mist! Giovanni wrapped a handkerchief about his hand and wondered what evil thing had stung him, and soon forgot his pain in a revery of Beatrice.

After the first interview, a second was in the inevitable course of what we call fate. A third; a fourth; and a meeting with Beatrice in the garden was no longer an incident in Giovanni's daily life, but the whole space in which he might be said to live; for the anticipation and memory of that ecstatic hour made up the remainder. Nor was it otherwise with the daughter of Rappaccini. She watched for the youth's appearance and flew to his side with confidence as unreserved as if they had been playmates from early infancy—as if they were such playmates still. If, by any unwonted chance, he failed to come at the appointed moment, she stood beneath the window and sent up the rich sweetness of her tones to float around him in his chamber and echo and reverberate throughout his heart. "Giovanni! Giovanni! Why tarriest thou? Come down!" And down he hastened into that Eden of poisonous flowers.

But, with all this intimate familiarity, there was still a reserve in Beatrice's demeanor, so rigidly and invariably sustained that the idea of infringing it scarcely occurred to his imagination. By all appreciable signs, they loved; they had looked love with eyes that conveyed the holy secret from the depths of one soul into the depths of the other, as if it were too sacred to be whispered by the way; they had even spoken love in those gushes of passion when their spirits darted forth in articulated breath like tongues of long hidden flame; and yet there had been no seal of lips, no clasp of hands, nor any slightest caress such as love claims and hallows. He had never touched one of the gleaming ringlets of her hair; her garment—so marked was the physical barrier between them—had never been waved against him by a breeze. On the few occasions when Giovanni had seemed tempted to overstep the limit, Beatrice grew so sad, so stern, and withal wore such a look of desolate separation, shuddering at itself, that not a spoken word was requisite to repel him. At such times he was startled at the horrible suspicions that rose, monster-like, out of the caverns of his heart and stared him in the face; his love grew thin and faint as the morning mist; his doubts alone had substance. But, when Beatrice's face brightened again after the momentary shadow, she was transformed at once from the mysterious, questionable being whom he had watched with so much awe and horror; she was now the beautiful and unsophisticated girl whom he felt that his spirit knew with a certainty beyond all other knowledge.

A considerable time had now passed since Giovanni's last meeting with Baglioni. One morning, however, he was disagreeably surprised by a visit from the professor, whom he had scarcely thought of for whole weeks, and would willingly have forgotten still longer. Given up as he had long been to a pervading excitement, he could tolerate no companions except upon condition of their perfect sympathy with his present state of feeling. Such sympathy was not to be expected from Professor Baglioni.

The visitor chatted carelessly for a few moments about the gossip of the city and the university, and then took up another topic.

"I have been reading an old classic author lately," said he, "and met with a story that strangely interested me. Possibly you may remember it. It is of an Indian prince, who sent a beautiful woman as a present to Alexander the Great. She was lovely as the dawn and gorgeous as the sunset; but what especially distinguished her was a certain rich perfume in her breath—richer than a garden of Persian roses. Alexander, as was natural to a youthful conqueror, fell in love at first sight with this magnificent stranger; but a certain sage physician, happening to be present, discovered a terrible secret in regard to her."

"And what was that?" asked Giovanni, turning his eyes downward to avoid those of the professor.

"That this lovely woman," continued Baglioni, with emphasis, "had been nourished with poisons from her birth upward, until her whole nature was so imbued with them that she herself had become the deadliest poison in existence. Poison was her element of life. With that rich perfume of her breath she blasted the very air. Her love would have been poison—her embrace death. Is not this a marvellous tale?"

"A childish fable," answered Giovanni, nervously starting from his chair. "I marvel how your worship finds time to read such nonsense among your graver studies."

"By the by," said the professor, looking uneasily about him, "what singular fragrance is this in your apartment? Is it the perfume of your gloves? It is faint, but delicious; and yet, after all, by no means agreeable. Were I to breathe it long, methinks it would make me ill. It is like the breath of a flower; but I see no flowers in the chamber."

"Nor are there any," replied Giovanni, who had turned pale as the professor spoke; "nor, I think, is there any fragrance except in your worship's imagination. Odors, being a sort of element combined of the sensual and the spiritual, are apt to deceive us in this manner. The recollection of a perfume, the bare idea of it, may easily be mistaken for a present reality."

"Ay; but my sober imagination does not often play such tricks," said Baglioni; "and, were I to fancy any kind of odor, it would be that of some vile apothecary drug, wherewith my fingers are likely enough to be imbued. Our worshipful friend Rappaccini, as I have heard, tinctures his medicaments with odors richer than those of Araby. Doubtless, likewise, the fair and learned Signora Beatrice would minister to her patients with draughts as sweet as a maiden's breath; but woe to him that sips them!"

Giovanni's face evinced many contradicting emotions. The tone in which the professor alluded to the pure and lovely daughter of Rappaccini was a torture to his soul; and yet the intimation of a view of her character, opposite to his own, gave instantaneous distinctness to a thousand dim suspicions, which now grinned at him like so many demons. But he strove hard to quell them and to respond to Baglioni with a true lover's perfect faith.

"Signor professor," said he, "you were my father's friend; perchance, too, it is your purpose to act a friendly part towards his son. I would fain feel nothing towards you save respect and deference; but I pray you to observe, signor, that there is one subject on which we must not speak. You know not the Signora Beatrice. You cannot, therefore, estimate the wrong—the blasphemy, I may even say—that is offered to her character by a light or injurious word."

"Giovanni! my poor Giovanni!" answered the professor, with a calm expression of pity, "I know this wretched girl far better than yourself. You shall hear the truth in respect to the poisoner Rappaccini and his poisonous daughter; yes, poisonous as she is beautiful. Listen; for, even should you do violence to my gray hairs, it shall not silence me. That old fable of the Indian woman has become a truth by the deep and deadly science of Rappaccini and in the person of the lovely Beatrice."

Giovanni groaned and hid his face.

"Her father," continued Baglioni, "was not restrained by natural affection from offering up his child in this horrible manner as the victim of his insane zeal for science; for, let us do him justice, he is as true a man of science as ever distilled his own heart in an alembic. What, then, will be your fate? Beyond a doubt you are selected as the material of some new experiment. Perhaps the result is to be death; perhaps a fate more awful still. Rappaccini, with what he calls the interest of science before his eyes, will hesitate at nothing."

"It is a dream," muttered Giovanni to himself; "surely it is a dream."

"But," resumed the professor, "be of good cheer, son of my friend. It is not yet too late for the rescue. Possibly we may even succeed in bringing back this miserable child within the limits of ordinary nature, from which her father's madness has estranged her. Behold this little silver vase! It was wrought by the hands of the renowned Benvenuto Cellini, and is well worthy to be a love gift to the fairest dame in Italy. But its contents are invaluable. One little sip of this antidote would have rendered the most virulent poisons of the Borgias innocuous. Doubt not that it will be as efficacious against those of Rappaccini. Bestow the vase, and the precious liquid within it, on your Beatrice, and hopefully await the result."

Baglioni laid a small, exquisitely wrought silver vial on the table and withdrew, leaving what he had said to produce its effect upon the young man's mind.

"We will thwart Rappaccini yet," thought he, chuckling to himself, as he descended the stairs; "but, let us confess the truth of him, he is a wonderful man— a wonderful man indeed; a vile empiric, however, in his practice, and therefore not to be tolerated by those who respect the good old rules of the medical profession."

Throughout Giovanni's whole acquaintance with Beatrice, he had occasionally, as we have said, been haunted by dark surmises as to her character; yet so thoroughly had she made herself felt by him as a simple, natural, most affectionate, and guileless creature, that the image now held up by Professor Baglioni looked as strange and incredible as if it were not in accordance with his own original conception. True, there were ugly recollections connected with his first glimpses of the beautiful girl; he could not quite forget the bouquet that withered in her grasp, and the insect that perished amid the sunny air, by no ostensible agency save the fragrance of her breath. These incidents, however, dissolving in the pure light of her character, had no longer the efficacy of facts, but were acknowledged as mistaken fantasies, by whatever testimony of the senses they might appear to be substantiated. There is something truer and more real than what we can see with the eyes and touch with the finger. On such better evidence had Giovanni founded his confidence in Beatrice, though rather by the necessary force of her high attributes than by any deep and generous faith on his part. But now his spirit was incapable of sustaining itself at the height to which the early enthusiasm of passion had exalted it; he fell down, grovelling among earthly doubts, and defiled therewith the pure whiteness of Beatrice's image. Not that he gave her up; he did but distrust. He resolved to institute some decisive test that should satisfy him, once for all, whether there were those dreadful peculiarities in her physical nature which could not be supposed to exist without some corresponding monstrosity of soul. His eyes, gazing down afar, might have deceived him as to the lizard, the insect, and the flowers; but if he could witness, at the distance of a few paces, the sudden blight of one fresh and healthful flower in Beatrice's hand, there would be room for no further question. With this idea he hastened to the florist's and purchased a bouquet that was still gemmed with the morning dewdrops.

It was now the customary hour of his daily interview with Beatrice. Before descending into the garden, Giovanni failed not to look at his figure in the mirror—a vanity to be expected in a beautiful young man, yet, as displaying itself at that troubled and feverish moment, the token of a certain shallowness of feeling and insincerity of character. He did gaze, however, and said to himself that his features had never before possessed so rich a grace, nor his eyes such vivacity, nor his cheeks so warm a hue of superabundant life.

"At least," thought he, "her poison has not yet insinuated itself into my system. I am no flower to perish in her grasp."

With that thought he turned his eyes on the bouquet, which he had never once laid aside from his hand. A thrill of indefinable horror shot through his frame on perceiving that those dewy flowers were already beginning to droop; they wore the aspect of things that had been fresh and lovely yesterday. Giovanni grew white as marble, and stood motionless before the mirror, staring at his own reflection there as at the likeness of something frightful. He remembered Baglioni's remark about the fragrance that seemed to pervade the chamber. It must have been the poison in his breath! Then he shuddered—shuddered at himself. Recovering from his stupor, he began to watch with curious eye a spider that was busily at work hanging its web from the antique cornice of the apartment, crossing and recrossing the artful system of interwoven lines—as vigorous and active a spider as ever dangled from an old ceiling. Giovanni bent towards the insect, and emitted a deep, long breath. The spider suddenly ceased its toil; the web vibrated with a tremor originating in the body of the small artisan. Again Giovanni sent forth a breath, deeper, longer, and imbued with a venomous feeling out of his heart: he knew not whether he were wicked, or only desperate. The spider made a convulsive gripe with his limbs and hung dead in the window.

"Accursed! accursed!" muttered Giovanni, addressing himself. "Hast thou grown so poisonous that this deadly insect perishes by thy breath?"

At that moment a rich, sweet voice came floating up from the garden.

"Giovanni! Giovanni! It is past the hour! Why tarriest thou? Come down!"

"Yes," muttered Giovanni again. "She is the only being whom my breath may not slay! Would that it might!"

He rushed down, and in an instant was standing before the bright and loving eyes of Beatrice. A moment ago his wrath and despair had been so fierce that he could have desired nothing so much as to wither her by a glance; but with her actual presence there came influences which had too real an existence to be at once shaken off; recollections of the delicate and benign power of her feminine nature, which had so often enveloped him in a religious calm; recollections of many a holy and passionate outrush of her heart, when the pure fountain had been unsealed from its depths and made visible in its transparency to his mental eye; recollections which, had Giovanni known how to estimate them, would have assured him that all this ugly mystery was but an earthly illusion, and that, whatever mist of evil might seem to have gathered over her, the real Beatrice was a heavenly angel. Incapable as he was of such high faith, still her presence had not utterly lost its magic. Giovanni's rage was quelled into an aspect of sullen insensibility. Beatrice, with a quick spiritual sense, immediately felt that there was a gulf of blackness between them which neither he nor she could pass. They walked on together, sad and silent, and came thus to the marble fountain and to its pool of water on the ground, in the midst of which grew the shrub that bore gemlike blossoms. Giovanni was affrighted at the eager enjoyment—the appetite, as it were—with which he found himself inhaling the fragrance of the flowers.

"Beatrice," asked he, abruptly, "whence came this shrub?"

"My father created it," answered she, with simplicity.

"Created it! created it!" repeated Giovanni. "What mean you, Beatrice?"

"He is a man fearfully acquainted with the secrets of nature," replied Beatrice; "and, at the hour when I first drew breath, this plant sprang from the soil, the offspring of his science, of his intellect, while I was but his earthly child. Approach it not!" continued she, observing with terror that Giovanni was drawing nearer to the shrub. "It has qualities that you little dream of. But I, dearest Giovanni,—I grew up and blossomed with the plant and was nourished with its breath. It was my sister, and I loved it with a human affection; for, alas!—hast thou not suspected it?—there was an awful doom."

Here Giovanni frowned so darkly upon her that Beatrice paused and trembled. But her faith in his tenderness reassured her, and made her blush that she had doubted for an instant.

"There was an awful doom," she continued, "The effect of my father's fatal love of science, which estranged me from all society of my kind. Until Heaven sent thee, dearest Giovanni, O, how lonely was thy poor Beatrice!"

"Was it a hard doom?" asked Giovanni, fixing his eyes upon her.

"Only of late have I known how hard it was," answered she, tenderly. "O, yes; but my heart was torpid, and therefore quiet."

Giovanni's rage broke forth from his sullen gloom like a lightning flash out of a dark cloud.

"Accursed one!" cried he, with venomous scorn and anger. "And, finding thy solitude wearisome, thou hast severed me likewise from all the warmth of life and enticed me into thy region of unspeakable horror!"

"Giovanni!" exclaimed Beatrice, turning her large bright eyes upon his face. The force of his words had not found its way into her mind; she was merely thunderstruck.

"Yes, poisonous thing!" repeated Giovanni, beside himself with passion. "Thou hast done it! Thou hast blasted me! Thou hast filled my veins with poison! Thou hast made me as hateful, as ugly, as loathsome and deadly a creature as thyself—a world's wonder of hideous monstrosity! Now, if our breath be happily as fatal to ourselves as to all others, let us join our lips in one kiss of unutterable hatred, and so die!"

"What has befallen me?" murmured Beatrice, with a low moan out of her heart. "Holy Virgin, pity me, a poor heart-broken child!"

"Thou,—dost thou pray?" cried Giovanni, still with the same fiendish scorn. "Thy very prayers, as they come from thy lips, taint the atmosphere with death. Yes, yes; let us pray! Let us to church and dip our fingers in the holy water at the portal! They that come after us will perish as by a pestilence! Let us sign crosses in the air! It will be scattering curses abroad in the likeness of holy symbols!"

"Giovanni," said Beatrice, calmly, for her grief was beyond passion, "why dost thou join thyself with me thus in those terrible words? I, it is true, am the horrible thing thou namest me. But thou,—what hast thou to do, save with one other shudder at my hideous misery to go forth out of the garden and mingle with thy race, and forget that there ever crawled on earth such a monster as poor Beatrice?"

"Dost thou pretend ignorance?" asked Giovanni, scowling upon her. "Behold! this power have I gained from the pure daughter of Rappaccini."

There was a swarm of summer insects flitting through the air in search of the food promised by the flower odors of the fatal garden. They circled round Giovanni's head, and were evidently attracted towards him by the same influence which had drawn them for an instant within the sphere of several of the shrubs. He sent forth a breath among them, and smiled bitterly at Beatrice as at least a score of the insects fell dead upon the ground.

"I see it! I see it!" shrieked Beatrice. "It is my father's fatal science! No, no, Giovanni; it was not I! Never! never! I dreamed only to love thee and be with thee a little time, and so to let thee pass away, leaving but thine image in mine heart; for, Giovanni, believe it, though my body be nourished with poison, my spirit is God's creature, and craves love as its daily food. But my father,—he has united us in this fearful sympathy. Yes; spurn me, tread upon me, kill me! O, what is death after such words as thine? But it was not I. Not for a world of bliss would I have done it."

Giovanni's passion had exhausted itself in its outburst from his lips. There now came across him a sense, mournful, and not without tenderness, of the intimate and peculiar relationship between Beatrice and himself. They stood, as it were, in an utter solitude, which would be made none the less solitary by the densest throng of human life. Ought not, then, the desert of humanity around them to press this insulated pair closer together? If they should be cruel to one another, who was there to be kind to them? Besides, thought Giovanni, might there not still be a hope of his returning within the limits of ordinary nature, and leading Beatrice, the redeemed Beatrice, by the hand? O, weak, and selfish, and unworthy spirit, that could dream of an earthly union and earthly happiness as possible, after such deep love had been so bitterly wronged as was Beatrice's love by Giovanni's blighting words! No, no; there could be no such hope. She must pass heavily, with that broken heart, across the borders of Time—she must bathe her hurt in some fount of paradise, and forget her grief in the light of immortality, and there be well.

But Giovanni did not know it.

"Dear Beatrice," said he, approaching her, while she shrank away as always at his approach, but now with a different impulse, "Dearest Beatrice, our fate is not yet so desperate. Behold! there is a medicine, potent, as a wise physician has assured me, and almost divine in its efficacy. It is composed of ingredients the most opposite to those by which thy awful father has brought this calamity upon thee and me. It is distilled of blessed herbs. Shall we not quaff it together, and thus be purified from evil?"

"Give it me!" said Beatrice, extending her hand to receive the little silver vial which Giovanni took from his bosom. She added, with a peculiar emphasis, "I will drink; but do thou await the result."

She put Baglioni's antidote to her lips; and, at the same moment, the figure of Rappaccini emerged from the portal and came slowly towards the marble fountain. As he drew near, the pale man of science seemed to gaze with a triumphant expression at the beautiful youth and maiden, as might an artist who should spend his life in achieving a picture or a group of statuary and finally be satisfied with his success. He paused; his bent form grew erect with conscious power; he spread out his hands over them in the attitude of a father imploring a blessing upon his children; but those were the same hands that had thrown poison into the stream of their lives. Giovanni trembled. Beatrice shuddered nervously, and pressed her hand upon her heart.

"My daughter," said Rappaccini, "thou art no longer lonely in the world. Pluck one of those precious gems from thy sister shrub and bid thy bridegroom wear it in his bosom. It will not harm him now. My science and the sympathy between thee and him have so wrought within his system that he now stands apart from common men, as thou dost, daughter of my pride and triumph, from ordinary women. Pass on, then, through the world, most dear to one another and dreadful to all besides!"

"My father," said Beatrice, feebly—and still as she spoke she kept her hand upon her heart,—"wherefore didst thou inflict this miserable doom upon thy child?"

"Miserable!" exclaimed Rappaccini. "What mean you, foolish girl? Dost thou

deem it misery to be endowed with marvellous gifts against which no power nor strength could avail an enemy—misery, to be able to quell the mightiest with a breath—misery, to be as terrible as thou art beautiful? Wouldst thou, then, have preferred the condition of a weak woman, exposed to all evil and capable of none?"

"I would fain have been loved, not feared," murmured Beatrice, sinking down upon the ground. "But now it matters not. I am going, father, where the evil which thou hast striven to mingle with my being will pass away like a dream—like the fragrance of these poisonous flowers, which will no longer taint my breath among the flowers of Eden. Farewell, Giovanni! Thy words of hatred are like lead within my heart; but they, too, will fall away as I ascend. O, was there not, from the first, more poison in thy nature than in mine?"

To Beatrice,—so radically had her earthly part been wrought upon by Rappaccini's skill,—as poison had been life, so the powerful antidote was death; and thus the poor victim of man's ingenuity and of thwarted nature, and of the fatality that attends all such efforts of perverted wisdom, perished there, at the feet of her father and Giovanni. Just at that moment Professor Pietro Baglioni looked forth from the window, and called loudly, in a tone of triumph mixed with horror, to the thunderstricken man of science,—

"Rappaccini! Rappaccini! and is *this* the upshot of your experiment?"

MAUD

Alfred, Lord Tennyson

PART I, XXII

I

COME INTO THE GARDEN, Maud,
    For the black bat, night, has flown,
Come into the garden, Maud,
    I am here at the gate alone;
And the woodbine spices are wafted abroad,
    And the musk of the rose is blown.

II

For a breeze of morning moves,
    And the planet of Love is on high,
Beginning to faint in the light that she loves
    On a bed of daffodil sky,
To faint in his light, and to die.

III

All night have the roses heard
    The flute, violin, bassoon;
All night has the casement jessamine stirr'd
    To the dancers dancing in tune;
Till a silence fell with the waking bird,
    And a hush with the setting moon.

IV

I said to the lily, "There is but one
    With whom she has heart to be gay.
When will the dancers leave her alone?
    She is weary of dance and play."
Now half to the setting moon are gone,
    And half to the rising day;
Low on the sand and loud on the stone
    The last wheel echoes away.

V

I said to the rose, "The brief night goes
    In babble and revel and wine.
O young lord-lover, what sighs are those,
    For one that will never be thine?
But mine, but mine," so I sware to the rose,
    "For ever and ever, mine."

VI

And the soul of the rose went into my blood,
    As the music clash'd in the hall;
And long by the garden lake I stood,
    For I heard your rivulet fall
From the lake to the meadow and on to the wood,
    Our wood, that is dearer than all;

VII

From the meadow your walks have left so sweet
    That whenever a March-wind sighs
He sets the jewel-print of your feet
    In violets blue as your eyes,
To the woody hollows in which we meet
    And the valleys of Paradise.

VIII

The slender acacia would not shake
    One long milk-bloom on the tree;

The white lake-blossom fell into the lake
 As the pimpernel dozed on the lea;
But the rose was awake all night for your sake,
 Knowing your promise to me;
The lilies and roses were all awake,
 They sigh'd for the dawn and thee.

IX

Queen rose of the rosebud garden of girls,
 Come hither, the dances are done,
In gloss of satin and glimmer of pearls,
 Queen lily and rose in one;
Shine out, little head, sunning over with curls,
 To the flowers, and be their sun.

X

There has fallen a splendid tear
 From the passion-flower at the gate.
She is coming, my dove, my dear;
 She is coming, my life, my fate;
The red rose cries, "She is near, she is near;"
 And the white rose weeps, "She is late;"
The larkspur listens, "I hear, I hear;"
 And the lily whispers, "I wait."

XI

She is coming, my own, my sweet;
 Were it ever so airy a tread,
My heart would hear her and beat,
 Were it earth in an earthy bed;
My dust would hear her and beat,
 Had I lain for a century dead;
Would start and tremble under her feet,
 And blossom in purple and red.

PART II, IV

I

O that 'twere possible
After long grief and pain
To find the arms of my true love
Round me once again!

II

When I was wont to meet her
In the silent woody places
By the home that gave me birth,
We stood tranced in long embraces
Mixt with kisses sweeter sweeter
Than anything on earth.

III

A shadow flits before me,
Not thou, but like to thee:
Ah Christ, that it were possible
For one short hour to see
The souls we loved, that they might tell us
What and where they be.

IV

It leads me forth at evening,
It lightly winds and steals
In a cold white robe before me,
When all my spirit reels
At the shouts, the leagues of lights,
And the roaring of the wheels.

V

Half the night I waste in sighs,
Half in dreams I sorrow after
The delight of early skies;
In a wakeful doze I sorrow

For the hand, the lips, the eyes,
For the meeting of the morrow,
The delight of happy laughter,
The delight of low replies.

VI

'Tis a morning pure and sweet,
And a dewy splendour falls
On the little flower that clings
To the turrets and the walls;
'Tis a morning pure and sweet,
And the light and shadow fleet;
She is walking in the meadow,
And the woodland echo rings;
In a moment we shall meet;
She is singing in the meadow
And the rivulet at her feet
Ripples on in light and shadow
To the ballad that she sings.

VII

Do I hear her sing as of old,
My bird with the shining head,
My own dove with the tender eye?
But there rings on a sudden a passionate cry,
There is some one dying or dead,
And a sullen thunder is roll'd;
For a tumult shakes the city,
And I wake, my dream is fled;
In the shuddering dawn, behold,
Without knowledge, without pity,
By the curtains of my bed
That abiding phantom cold.

VIII

Get thee hence, nor come again,
Mix not memory with doubt,
Pass, thou deathlike type of pain,
Pass and cease to move about!
'Tis the blot upon the brain
That will show itself without.

IX

Then I rise, the eavedrops fall,
And the yellow vapours choke
The great city sounding wide;
The day comes, a dull red ball
Wrapt in drifts of lurid smoke
On the misty river-tide.

X

Thro' the hubbub of the market
I steal, a wasted frame,
It crosses here, it crosses there,
Thro' all that crowd confused and loud,
The shadow still the same;
And on my heavy eyelids
My anguish hangs like shame.

XI

Alas for her that met me,
That heard me softly call,
Came glimmering thro' the laurels
At the quiet evenfall,
In the garden by the turrets
Of the old manorial hall.

XII

Would the happy spirit descend,
From the realms of light and song,
In the chamber or the street,

As she looks among the blest,
Should I fear to greet my friend
Or to say 'Forgive the wrong,'
Or to ask her, 'Take me, sweet,
To the regions of thy rest'?

XIII

But the broad light glares and beats,
And the shadow flits and fleets
And will not let me be;
And I loathe the squares and streets,
And the faces that one meets,
Hearts with no love for me:
Always I long to creep
Into some still cavern deep,
There to weep, and weep, and weep
My whole soul out to thee.

PART II, V

VIII

But I know where a garden grows,
Fairer than aught in the world beside,
All made up of the lily and rose
That blow by night, when the season is good,
To the sound of dancing music and flutes:
It is only flowers, they had no fruits,
And I almost fear they are not roses, but blood;
For the keeper was one, so full of pride,
He linkt a dead man there to a spectral bride;
For he, if he had not been a Sultan of brutes,
Would he have that hole in his side?

IX

But what will the old man say?
he laid a cruel snare in a pit

To catch a friend of mine one stormy day;
Yet now I could even weep to think of it;
For what will the old man say
When he comes to the second corpse in the pit?

X

Friend, to be struck by the public foe,
Then to strike him and lay him low,
That were public merit, far,
Whatever the Quaker holds, from sin;
But the red life spilt for a private blow—
I swear to you, lawful and lawless war
Are scarcely even akin.

XI

O me, why have they not buried me deep enough?
Is it kind to have made me a grave so rough,
Me, that was never a quiet sleeper?
Maybe still I am but half-dead;
Then I cannot be wholly dumb;
I will cry to the steps above my head
And somebody, surely, some kind heart will come
To bury me, bury me
Deeper, ever so little deeper.

Gardens of the MIND

THE SCARLET FLOWER

Vsevolod Garshin

HE WAS AWARE that he was in a mental hospital; he was even aware that he was ill. Occasionally, as on the first night, he woke up in the stillness of the night after a whole day of turbulent movement, aching in all his limbs and with a terrible heaviness in his head, but he would be fully conscious. Possibly it was due to the absence of sensory stimuli in the nocturnal silence and the semi-darkness, or perhaps the reduced functioning of his brain on waking, but at such moments he understood his situation clearly and was more or less normal. But with the coming of day and the wakening of life in the hospital all those sensations would again wash over him; his sick brain could not cope and he would be insane again. His condition was a strange blend of correct judgements and preposterous notions. He realized that all those around him were sick people, yet at the same time he saw some other person hidden or trying to hide himself in every one of them, someone he had known before or someone he had read or heard about. The hospital was populated by people from all times and from all lands. Here were both the living and the dead. Here were the famous and the mighty of the world as well as ordinary soldiers killed in the last war and risen from the dead. He saw himself in some magic enchanted circle that had gathered within itself all the might of the earth, and in an ecstasy of pride, he regarded himself as the centre of that circle. All of them, his fellow inmates, had fore-gathered here in order to carry out a task which he dimly conceived of as a gigantic venture aimed at the destruction of evil on earth. He did not know what form this task would take, but he felt enough strength to carry it out. He could read the thoughts of other men; he saw in objects their own history; the large elm tree in the hospital grounds told him whole legends from the past; he believed that the building, which had in fact been built some time ago, dated back to Peter the Great and he was certain that the Tsar had lived in it at the time of the Battle of Poltava. He could read this in the walls, in the crumbling plaster, on bits of brick and tiles that he found in the grounds; the entire history of the house and the grounds was written on them. He populated the little mortuary with dozens, hundreds, of men long dead and he would stare into the little basement window opening on to the secluded corner of the grounds, and in the light unevenly reflected in the old and dirty rainbow-coloured pane he saw familiar faces that he had once seen in life or in portraits.

Meanwhile fine, bright weather had set in; the patients were spending whole days out of doors in the grounds. Their part of the grounds was rather small but it was thickly planted with trees, and flowers grew in every possible place. The supervisor allocated gardening tasks to everybody who was at all capable of doing any work; for whole days they swept the paths and strewed sand on them, weeded and watered the flowerbeds, the cucumber, water-melon and melon patches that had all been dug and planted by their own hands. In one corner of the garden there were many cherry trees close together; alongside there was an avenue of elms; in the middle, on a small artificial mound, a flowerbed had been laid out, the most beautiful one in the whole garden; there were bright flowers around the edges of the highest part of the mound and its centre was occupied by a rare and magnificent dahlia which had large yellow petals flecked with red. It was also the centre of the garden as a whole, rising above it, and one could see that many of the patients attributed some mystical significance to it. The new patient, too, thought that it was something out of the ordinary, a Guardian Goddess of the grounds and the building. The inmates had also planted flowers along all the paths. Here were all the flowers that one would encounter in Ukrainian gardens: standard roses, bright petunias, tall tobacco plants with their small pink blossoms, mint, marigolds, nasturtiums and poppies. Not far from the porch there were three poppy plants of some special variety; they were much smaller than the ordinary ones and also differed from them by the exceptional brilliance of their scarlet colouring. It was this flower that had so struck him when on his first day at the hospital he had been looking out at the ground through the french window.

When he went into the garden for the first time he looked first at these brilliant flowers before descending the steps. There were only two of them then; it so happened that they grew apart from the other flowers on an unweeded spot, surrounded by dense goosefoot and some kind of steppe grass.

One by one the patients came through the door where the warder handed each of them a thick white knitted cap with a red cross on the forehead. These caps had been used in the war and had been bought at an auction. But, needless to say, the Patient attributed a special, mystical significance to this cross. He took off the cap, looked at the cross and then at the poppies. The flowers were brighter.

"He's winning," said the Patient, "but we shall see."

And he stepped down from the porch. Though he looked round, he did not notice the orderly standing behind him, and he stepped across the flower bed and stretched his hand towards the flower, but could not bring himself to pick it. He felt a sensation of heat and stabbing in his outstretched hand and then in his whole body, as though some powerful current of a force unknown to him emanated from the red petals and permeated his entire body. He moved closer and stretched his hand quite close to the flower, but it seemed to him that the flower was defending itself by emitting a deadly, venomous breath. His head began to spin; he made one desperate, final effort and had already grasped the stalk when suddenly a heavy hand was laid on his shoulder. The orderly had caught hold of him.

"You mustn't pick the flowers," said the old Ukrainian. "And don't step on the flower beds. There's lots of you lunatics here: if every one of you picks a flower you'll soon have stripped the whole garden." He spoke earnestly, still holding the Patient's shoulder.

The Patient looked him in the face, freed himself silently from his grip and walked along the path in an agitated state. "Oh you unhappy ones!" he thought. "You can't see, you've become so blind, that you even protect him. But I'll finish him off, come what may. If not today, then tomorrow we'll measure our strength against each other. And does it really matter if I perish . . . ?"

He walked around the garden until evening, meeting other inmates and engaging them in weird conversations, in which each speaker heard only answers to his own insane thoughts expressed in absurd, mysterious words. The Patient walked first with one inmate and then with another, and by the end of the day he was even more convinced that "all was ready," as he said himself. Soon, soon, the iron bars will fall asunder and all those imprisoned here will go out and rush to all the corners of the earth, and the whole world will shudder, cast off its shabby old covering and will appear in a splendid new beauty. He had all but forgotten about the flower, but as he left the garden and mounted the steps to the porch he saw what looked like two red pieces of coal in the thick grass that had already darkened and was becoming dewy. Then the Patient lingered behind the crowd, positioned himself behind the orderly and waited for a suitable moment. Nobody saw him jump across the flowerbed, seize the flower and hurriedly hide it on his chest under his shirt. When the cool, damp leaves touched his body, he turned pale as death and his eyes opened wide in terror. A cold sweat broke out on his forehead.

The lamps were lit in the hospital; most of the inmates lay down on their beds, waiting for supper, apart from a few restless ones who strode hurriedly about the corridor and the wards. Among them was the Patient with the flower. He walked about with his arms convulsively pressed crosswise over his chest: it seemed as if he wanted to crush and squash the plant that lay hidden there. When he met other inmates, he would give them a wide berth, afraid that the edge of his gown might touch them. "Keep away, keep away!" he would shout. But in the hospital few people took any notice of such exclamations. And he walked faster and faster, making his strides bigger and bigger, and he walked for an hour, two hours, in a frenzied state.

"I'll wear you out. I'll strangle you!" he kept saying in a toneless and malicious voice.

At times he would grind his teeth.

Supper was served in the dining-hall. A thin millet gruel was served in the few wooden, painted and gilded bowls that stood on the large, bare tables; the patients took their seats on the benches; each was given a hunk of black bread. They ate with wooden spoons, about eight men eating straight from each bowl. A few who were on an improved diet were served separately. Our Patient gulped down his portion which the orderly brought to him in his room where he had been told to go; but he was not content with this and went into the dining-room.

"May I sit down here?" he asked the supervisor.

"Haven't you had your supper?" The supervisor was pouring extra helpings of gruel into the bowls.

"I'm very hungry. And I have to build up my strength as much as I can. Food is my only support; you know I don't sleep at all."

"Help yourself, my friend, and may it do you good. Taras, give him a spoon and some bread."

He sat near one of the bowls and ate an enormous amount of gruel.

"That will do now, surely, that will do," said the supervisor at last when everybody had finished his supper, but our Patient was still sitting at the bowl, spooning gruel with one hand and clutching his chest with the other. "You'll over-eat yourself."

"Ah, if only you knew how much strength I need, how much strength! Goodbye, Nikolay Nikolaich," said the Patient, getting up from the table and squeezing the supervisor's hand with all his strength. "Good-bye."

"Where are you off to?" the supervisor asked with a smile.

"Me? Nowhere. I'm staying. But maybe tomorrow we shan't be seeing each other again. Thank you for all your kindness."

Once more he shook the supervisor's hand firmly. His voice was trembling and tears sprang to his eyes.

"Calm yourself, my friend, calm yourself," replied the supervisor. "Why these gloomy thoughts? You go and lie down and have a good sleep. You really ought to sleep more; once you sleep properly, you'll soon get better."

The Patient was sobbing. The supervisor had turned away to tell the orderlies to hurry up and clear away what was left of the supper. Half an hour later all were asleep in the hospital, except for one man, who lay fully clothed on his bed in the corner room. He was shivering as in a fever and was convulsively clutching his chest which was, as he believed, impregnated by an unknown, deadly poison.

THE GARDEN
OF FORKING PATHS

Jorge Luis Borges

ON PAGE 22 of Liddell Hart's *History of World War I* you will read that an attack against the Serre-Montauban line by thirteen British divisions (supported by 1,400 artillery pieces), planned for 24 July 1916, had to be postponed until the morning of the 29th. The torrential rains, Captain Liddell Hart comments, caused this delay, an insignificant one, to be sure.

The following statement, dictated, reread and signed by Dr Yu Tsun, former professor of English at the *Hochschule* at Tsingtao, throws an unsuspected light over the whole affair. The first two pages of the document are missing.

. . . and I hung up the receiver. Immediately afterwards, I recognized the voice that had answered in German. It was that of Captain Richard Madden. Madden's presence in Viktor Runeberg's apartment meant the end of our anxieties and—but this seemed, or *should have seemed,* very secondary to me—also the end of our lives. It meant that Runeberg had been arrested or murdered.* Before the sun set on that day, I would encounter the same fate. Madden was implacable. Or rather, he was obliged to be so. An Irishman at the service of England, a man accused of laxity and perhaps of treason, how could he fail to seize and be thankful for such a miraculous opportunity: the discovery, capture, maybe even the death of two agents of the German Reich? I went up to my room; absurdly I locked the door and threw myself on my back on the narrow iron cot. Through the window I saw the familiar roofs and

---

*An hypothesis both hateful and odd. The Prussian spy Hans Rabener, alias Viktor Runeberg, attacked with drawn automatic the bearer of the warrent for his arrest, Captain Richard Madden. The latter, in self-defence, inflicted the wound which brought about Runeberg's death. (Editor's note, from the original text.)

the cloud-shaded six o'clock sun. It seemed incredible to me that that day without premonitions of symbols should be the one of my inexorable death. In spite of my dead father, in spite of having been a child in a symmetrical garden of Hai Feng, was I—now—going to die? Then I reflected that everything happens to a man precisely, precisely now. Centuries of centuries and only in the present do things happen; countless men in the air, on the face of the earth and the sea, and all that really is happening is happening to me . . . The almost intolerable recollection of Madden's horse-like face banished these wanderings. In the midst of my hatred and terror (it means nothing to me now to speak of terror, now that I have mocked Richard Madden, now that my throat yearns for the noose) it occurred to me that that tumultuous and doubtless happy warrior did not suspect that I possessed the Secret. The name of the exact location of the new British artillery park on the River Ancre. A bird streaked across the grey sky and blindly I translated it into an aeroplane and that aeroplane into many (against the French sky) annihilating the artillery station with vertical bombs. If only my mouth, before a bullet shattered it, could cry out that secret name so it could be heard in Germany . . . My human voice was very weak. How might I make it carry to the ear of the Chief? To the ear of that sick and hateful man who knew nothing of Runeberg and me save that we were in Staffordshire and who was waiting in vain for our report in his arid office in Berlin, endlessly examining newspapers . . . I said out loud: *I must flee*. I sat up noiselessly, in a useless perfection of silence, as if Madden were already lying in wait for me. Something—perhaps the mere vain ostentation of proving my resources were nil—made me look through my pockets. I found what I knew I would find. The American watch, the nickel chain and the square coin, the key ring with the incriminating useless keys to Runeberg's apartment, the notebook, a letter which I resolved to destroy immediately (and which I did not destroy), a crown, two shillings and a few pence, the red and blue pencil, the handkerchief, the revolver with one bullet. Absurdly, I took it in my hand and weighed it in order to inspire courage within myself. Vaguely I thought that a pistol report can be heard at a great distance. In ten minutes my plan was perfected. The telephone book listed the name of the only person capable of transmitting the message; he lived in a suburb of Fenton, less than a half hour's train ride away.

I am a cowardly man. I say it now, now that I have carried to its end a plan whose perilous nature no one can deny. I know its execution was terrible. I didn't do it for Germany, no. I care nothing for a barbarous country which imposed upon me the abjection of being a spy. Besides, I know of a man from England—a modest man—who for me is no less great that Goethe. I talked with him for scarcely an hour, but during that hour he was Goethe . . . I did it because I sensed that the Chief somehow feared people of my race—for the innumerable ancestors who merge within me. I wanted to prove to him that a yellow man could save his armies.

Besides, I had to flee from Captain Madden. His hands and his voice could call at my door at any moment. I dressed silently, bade farewell to myself in the mirror, went downstairs, scrutinized the peaceful street and went out. The station was not far from my home, but I judged it wise to take a cab. I argued that in this way I ran less risk of being recognized; the fact is that in the deserted street I felt myself visible and vulnerable, infinitely so. I remember that I told the cab driver to stop a short distance before the main entrance. I got out with voluntary, almost painful slowness; I was going to the village of Ashgrove but I bought a ticket for a more distant station. The train left within a very few minutes, at eight-fifty. I hurried; the next one would leave at nine-thirty. There was hardly a soul on the platform. I went through the coaches; I remember a few farmers, a woman dressed in mourning, a young boy who was reading with fervour the *Annals* of Tacitus, a wounded and happy soldier. The coaches jerked forward at last. A man whom I recognized ran in vain to the end of the platform. It was Captain Richard Madden. Shattered, trembling, I shrank into the far corner of the seat, away from the dreaded window.

From this broken state I passed into an almost abject felicity. I told myself that the duel had already begun and that I had won the first encounter by frustrating, even if for forty minutes, even if by a stroke of fate, the attack of my adversary. I argued that this slightest of victories foreshadowed a total victory. I argued (no less fallaciously) that my cowardly felicity proved that I was a man capable of carrying out the adventure successfully. From this weakness I took strength that did not abandon me. I foresee that man will resign himself each day to more atrocious undertakings; soon there will be no one but warriors and brigands; I give them this counsel: *The author of an atrocious undertaking ought to imagine that he has already accomplished it, ought to impose upon himself a future as irrevocable as the past.* Thus I proceeded as my eyes of a man already dead registered the elapsing of that day, which was perhaps the last, and the diffusion of the night. The train ran gently along, amid ash trees. It stopped, almost in the middle of the fields. No one announced the name of the station. "Ashgrove?" I asked a few lads on the platform. "Ashgrove," they replied. I got off.

A lamp enlightened the platform but the faces of the boys were in shadow. One questioned me, "Are you going to Dr Stephen Albert's house?" Without waiting for my answer, another said, "The house is a long way from here, but you won't get lost if you take this road to the left and at every crossroads turn again to your left." I tossed them a coin (my last), descended a few stone steps and stared down the solitary road. It went downhill, slowly. It was of elemental earth; overhead the branches were tangled; the low full moon seemed to accompany me.

For an instant, I thought that Richard Madden in some way had penetrated my desperate plan. Very quickly, I understood that that was impossible. The instructions to turn always to the left reminded me that such was the common procedure for discovering the central point of certain labyrinths. I have some understanding of labyrinths: not for nothing am I the great grandson of that Ts'ui Pên who was governor of Yunnan and who renounced worldly power in order to write a novel that might be even more populous than the Hung Lu Meng and to construct a labyrinth in which all men would become lost. Thirteen years he dedicated to these heterogeneous tasks, but the hand of a stranger murdered him—and his novel was incoherent and no one found the labyrinth. Beneath English trees I meditated on that lost maze: I imagined it inviolate and perfect at the secret crest of a mountain; I imagined it erased by rice fields or beneath the water; I imagined it infinite, no longer composed of octagonal kiosks and returning paths, but of rivers and provinces and kingdoms . . . I thought of a labyrinth of labyrinths, of one sinuous spreading labyrinth that would encompass the past and the future and in some way involve the stars. Absorbed in these illusory images, I forgot my destiny of one pursued. I felt myself to be, for an unknown period of time, an abstract perceiver of the world. The vague, living countryside, the moon, the remains of the day worked on me, as well as the slope of the road which eliminated any possibility of weariness. The afternoon was intimate, infinite. The road descended and forked among the now confused meadows. A high-pitched, almost syllabic music approached and receded in the shifting of the wind, dimmed by leaves and distance. I thought that a man can be an enemy of other men, of the moments of other men, but not of a country: not of fireflies, words, gardens, streams of water, sunsets. Thus I arrived before a tall, rusty gate. Between the iron bars I made out a poplar grove and a pavilion. I understood suddenly two things, the first trivial, the second almost unbelievable: the music came from the pavilion, and the music was Chinese. For precisely that reason I had openly accepted it without paying it any heed. I do not remember whether there was a bell or whether I knocked with my hand. The sparkling of the music continued.

From the rear of the house within a lantern approached: a lantern that the trees sometimes striped and sometimes eclipsed, a paper lantern that had the form of a drum and the colour of the moon. A tall man bore it. I didn't see his face for the light blinded me. He opened the door and said slowly, in my own language: "I see that the pious Hsi P'êng persists in correcting my solitude. You no doubt wish to see the garden?"

I recognized the name of one of our consuls and I replied, disconcerted, "The garden?"

"The garden of forking paths."

Something stirred in my memory and I uttered with incomprehensible certainty, "The garden of my ancestor Ts'ui Pên."

"Your ancestor? Your illustrious ancestor? Come in."

The damp path zigzagged like those of my childhood. We came to a library of Eastern and Western books. I recognized bound in yellow silk several volumes of the Lost Encyclopaedia, edited by the Third Emperor of the Luminous Dynasty but never printed. The record on the phonograph revolved next to a bronze phoenix. I also recall a *famille* rose vase and another, many centuries older, of that shade of blue which our craftsmen copied from the otters of Persia . . .

Stephen Albert observed me with a smile. He was, as I have said, very tall, sharp-featured, with grey eyes and a grey beard. He told me that he had been a missionary in Tientsin "before aspiring to become a Sinologist."

We sat down—I on a long, low divan, he with his back to the window and a tall circular clock. I calculated that my pursuer, Richard Madden, could not arrive for at least an hour. My irrevocable determination could wait.

"An astounding fate, that of Ts'ui Pên," Stephen Albert said. "Governor of his native province, learned in astronomy, in astrology and in the tireless interpretation of the canonical books, chess player, famous poet and calligrapher—he abandoned all this in order to compose a book and a maze. He renounced the pleasures of both tyranny and justice, of his populous couch, of his banquets and even of erudition—all to close himself up for thirteen years in the Pavilion of the Limpid Solitude. When he died, his heirs found nothing save chaotic manuscripts. His family, as you may be aware, wished to condemn them to the fire, but his executor—a Taoist or Buddhist monk—insisted on their publication."

"We descendants of Ts'ui Pên," I replied, "continue to curse that monk. Their publication was senseless. The book is an indeterminate heap of contradictory drafts. I examined it once: in the third chapter the hero dies, in the fourth he is alive. As for the other undertaking of Ts'ui Pên, his labyrinth . . ."

"Here is Ts'ui Pên's labyrinth," he said, indicating a tall lacquered desk.

"An ivory labyrinth!" I exclaimed. "A minimum labyrinth."

"A labyrinth of symbols," he corrected. "An invisible labyrinth of time. To me, a barbarous Englishman, has been entrusted the revelation of this diaphanous mystery. After more than a hundred years, the details are irretrievable; but it is not hard to conjecture what happened. Ts'ui Pên must have said once: *I am withdrawing to write a book.* And another time: *I am withdrawing to construct a labyrinth.* Every one imagined two works; to no one did it occur that the book and the maze were one and the same thing. The Pavilion of the Limpid Solitude stood in the centre of a garden that was perhaps intricate; that circumstance could have suggested to the heirs a physical labyrinth. Ts'ui Pên died; no one in the vast territories that were his came upon the labyrinth; the confusion of the novel suggested to me that it was the maze. Two circumstances gave me the correct solution of the problem. One: the curious legend that Ts'ui Pên had planned to create a labyrinth which would be strictly infinite. The other: a fragment of a letter I discovered."

Albert rose. He turned his back on me for a moment; he opened a drawer of the black and gold desk. He faced me and in his hands he held a sheet of paper that had once been crimson, but was now pink and tenuous and cross-sectioned. The fame of Ts'ui Pên as a calligrapher had been justly won. I read, uncomprehendingly and with fervour, these words written with a minute brush by a man of my blood: *I leave to the various futures (not to all) my garden of forking paths.* Wordlessly, I returned the sheet. Albert continued:

"Before unearthing this letter, I had questioned myself about the ways in which the book can be infinite. I could think of nothing other than a cyclic volume, a circular one. A book whose last page was identical with the first, a book which had the possibility of continuing indefinitely. I remembered too that night which is at the middle of the Thousand and One Nights when Scheherazade (through a magical oversight of the copyist) begins to relate word for word the story of the Thousand and One Nights, establishing the risk of coming once again to the night when she must repeat it, and thus on to infinity. I imagined as well a Platonic, hereditary work, transmitted from father to son, in which each new individual adds a chapter or corrects with pious care the pages of his elders. These conjectures diverted me; but none seemed to correspond, not even remotely, to the contradictory chapters of Ts'ui Pên. In the midst of this perplexity, I received from Oxford the manuscript you have examined. I lingered, naturally, on the sentence: *I leave to the various futures (not to all) my garden of forking paths.* Almost instantly, I understood: 'the garden of forking paths' was the chaotic novel; the phrase 'the various futures (not to all)' suggested to me the forking in time, not in space. A broad rereading of the work confirmed the theory. In all fictional works, each time a man is confronted with several alternatives, he chooses one and eliminates the others; in the fiction of Ts'ui Pên, he chooses—simultaneously—all of them. He creates, in this way, diverse futures, diverse times which themselves also proliferate and fork. Here, then, is the explanation of the novel's contradictions. Fang, let us say, has a secret; a stranger calls at his door; Fang resolves to kill him. Naturally, there are several possible outcomes: Fang can kill the intruder, the intruder can kill Fang, they both can escape, they both can die, and so forth. In the work of Ts'ui Pên, all possible outcomes occur; each one is the point of departure for other forkings. Sometimes, the paths of this labyrinth converge: for example, you arrive at this house, but in one of the possible pasts you are my enemy, in another, my friend. If you will resign yourself to my incurable pronunciation, we shall read a few pages."

His face, within the vivid circle of the lamplight, was unquestionably that of an old man, but with something unalterable about it, even immortal. He read with slow precision two versions of the same epic chapter. In the first, an army marches to a battle across a lonely mountain; the horror of the rocks and shadows makes the men undervalue their lives and they gain an easy victory. In the second, the same army traverses a palace where a great festival is taking place; the resplendent battle seems to them a continuation of the celebration and they win the victory. I listened with proper veneration to these ancient narratives, perhaps less admirable in themselves than the fact that they had been created by my blood and were being restored to me by a man of remote empire, in the course of a desperate adventure, on a Western isle. I remember the last words, repeated in each version like a secret commandment: *Thus fought the heroes, tranquil their admirable hearts, violent their swords, resigned to kill and to die.*

From that moment on, I felt about me and within my dark body an invisible, intangible swarming. Not the swarming of the divergent, parallel and finally coalescent armies, but a more inaccessible, more intimate agitation that they in some manner prefigured. Stephen Albert continued:

"I don't believe that your illustrious ancestor played idly with these variations. I don't consider it credible that he would sacrifice thirteen years to the infinite execution of a rhetorical experiment. In your country, the novel is a subsidiary form of literature; in Ts'ui Pên's time it was a despicable form. Ts'ui Pên was a brilliant novelist, but he was also a man of letters who doubtless did not consider himself a mere novelist. The testimony of his contemporaries proclaims—and his life fully confirms—his metaphysical and mystical interests. Philosophic controversy usurps a good part of the novel. I know that of all problems, none disturbed him so greatly nor worked upon him so much as the abysmal problem of time. Now then, the latter is the only problem that does not figure in the pages of the *Garden*. He does not even use the word that signifies time. How do you explain this voluntary omission?"

I proposed several solutions—all unsatisfactory. We discussed them. Finally Stephen Albert said to me:

"In a riddle whose answer is chess, what is the only prohibited word?"

I thought a moment and replied, "The word *chess*."

"Precisely," said Albert. "*The Garden of Forking Paths* is an enormous riddle, or parable, whose theme is time; this recondite cause prohibits its mention. To omit a word always, to resort to inept metaphors and obvious periphrases, is perhaps the most emphatic way of stressing it. That is the tortuous method preferred, in each of the meanderings of his indefatigable novel, by the oblique Ts'ui Pên. I have compared hundreds of manuscripts, I have corrected the errors that the negligence of the copyists has introduced, I have guessed the plan of this chaos, I have re-established—I believe I have re-established—the primordial organization, I have translated the entire work: it is clear to me that not once does he employ the word 'time'. The explanation is obvious: *The Garden of Forking Paths* is an incomplete, but not false, image of the universe as Ts'ui Pên conceived it. In contrast to Newton and Schopenhauer, your ancestor did not believe in a uniform, absolute time. He believed in an infinite series of times, in a growing, dizzying net of divergent, convergent and parallel times. This network of times which approached one another, forked, broke off, or were unaware of one another for centuries, embraces *all* possibilities of time. We do not exist in the majority of these times; in some you exist, and not I; in others I, and not you; in others, both of us. In the present one, which a favourable fate has granted me, you have arrived at my house; in another, while crossing the garden, you found me dead; in still another, I utter these same words, but I am a mistake, a ghost."

"In every one," I pronounced, not without a tremble to my voice, "I am grateful to you and revere you for your re-creation of the garden of Ts'ui Pên."

"Not in all," he murmured with a smile. "Time forks perpetually towards innumerable futures. In one of them I am your enemy."

Once again I felt the swarming sensation of which I have spoken. It seemed to me that the humid garden that surrounded the house was infinitely saturated with invisible persons. Those persons were Albert and I, secret, busy and multiform in other dimensions of time. I raised my eyes and the tenuous nightmare dissolved. In the yellow and black garden there was only one man; but this man was as strong as a statue . . . this man was approaching along the path and he was Captain Richard Madden.

"The future already exists," I replied, "but I am your friend. Could I see the letter again?"

Albert rose. Standing tall, he opened the drawer of the tall desk; for the moment his back was to me. I had readied the revolver. I fired with extreme caution. Albert fell uncomplainingly, immediately. I swear his death was instantaneous—a lightning stroke.

The rest is unreal, insignificant. Madden broke in, arrested me. I have been condemned to the gallows. I have won out abominably; I have communicated to Berlin the secret name of the city they must attack. They bombed it yesterday; I read it in the same papers that offered to England the mystery of the learned Sinologist Stephen Albert who was murdered by a stranger, one Yu Tsun. The Chief had deciphered this mystery. He knew my problem was to indicate (through the uproar of the war) the city called Albert, and that I had found no other means to do so than to kill a man of that name. He does not know (no one can know) my innumerable contrition and weariness.

132

A TALE OF TWO GARDENS

Octavio Paz

A HOUSE, a garden,
                              are not places:
they spin, they come and go.
                                        Their apparitions open
another space
                    in space,
another time in time.
                              Their eclipses
are not abdications:
the vivacity of one of those moments
                                                  would burn us
if it lasted a moment more.
                                        We are condemned
to kill time:
                    so we die,
little by little.
                    A garden is not a place.
Down a path of reddish sand,
we enter a drop of water,

drink green clarities from its center,
we climb
                    the spiral of hours
to the tip of the day,
                              descend
to the last burning of its ember.
Mumbling river,
                        the garden flows through the night.

That one in Mixcoac, abandoned,
covered with scars,
                        was a body
at the point of collapse.
                              I was a boy,
and the garden for me was like a grandfather.
I clambered up its leafy knees,
not knowing it was doomed.
The garden knew it:
                        it awaited its destruction
as a condemned man awaits the axe.
The fig tree was a goddess,
                              the Mother.
Hum of irascible insects,
the muffled drums of the blood,
the sun and its hammer,
the green hug of innumerable limbs.
The cleft in the trunk:
                              the world half-opened.
I thought I had seen death:
                              I saw
the other face of being,
                              the feminine void,
the fixed featureless splendor.

White leagues batter
the crest of Ajusco,
                    turn black,
a purple mass,
                a great bulge splitting open:
the rainsquall's gallop covers the plain.
Rain on lava:
              the water dances
on bloodstained stone.
                      Light, light:
the stuff of time and its inventions.
Months like mirrors,
one by the other reflected and effaced.
Days when nothing happens,
studying an ants' nest,
its subterranean labor,
its fierce rites.
                  Immersed in the cruel light,
I washed my ants' nest body,
                      I watched
the restless construction of my ruin.
Elytra:
            the insect's razor song
slices the dry grass.

                Mineral cacti,
quicksilver lizards in adobe walls,
the bird that drills through space,
thirst, tedium, clouds of dust,
impalpable epiphanies of wind.
The pines taught me to talk to myself.
In that garden I learned to wave myself goodbye.

Later there were no gardens.

One day,

as if I had returned,

not to my house,

but to the beginning of the Beginning,

I reached a clarity.

Space made of air

for the passionate games

of water and light.

Diaphanous convergences:

from the twittering of green

to the most humid blue

to the grey of embers

to a woundlike pink

to an unburied gold.

I heard a dark green murmur

burst from the center of the night: the neem tree.

On its shoulders,

the sky

with all its barbarian jewels.

The heat was a huge closing hand,

one could hear the roots panting,

space expanding,

the crumbling of the year.

The tree would not give way.

Huge as a monument to patience,

fair as the balance that weighs

a dewdrop,

a grain of light,

an instant.

Many moons fit in its branches.

House of squirrels,

blackbird inn.

Strength is fidelity,

power reverence:

no one ends at himself,

                        each one is an all

in another all,

                in another one.

The other is contained in the one,

                            the one is another:

we are constellations.

                   The enormous neem

once knew how to be small.

                     At its feet

I knew I was alive,

                I knew

that death is expansion,

                    self-negation is growth.

I learned,

            in the brotherhood of the trees,

to reconcile myself,

                  not with myself:

with what lifts me, sustains me, lets me fall.

I crossed paths with a girl.

                  Her eyes:

the pact between the summer and the autumn suns.

She was a follower of acrobats, astronomers, camel drivers.

I of lighthouse keepers, logicians, saddhus.

                                Our bodies

spoke, mingled, and went off.

We went off with them.

                    It was the monsoon.

Skies of grass-bits

              and armed wind

at the crossroads.

              I named her Almendrita

after the girl of the story,

sailor of a stormy pond.

                Not a name:

an intrepid sailboat.

It rained,
the earth dressed and became naked,
snakes left their holes,
the moon was made of water,

the sun was water,
the sky took out its braids
and its braids were unraveled rivers,
the rivers swallowed villages,
death and life were jumbled,
dough of mud and sun,
season of lust and plague,
season of lightning on a sandalwood tree,
mutilated genital stars

rotting,
reviving in your womb,

mother India,
girl India,
drenched in semen, sap, poisons, juices.

Scales grew on the house.

Almendrita:
flame intact through the snaking and the wind-gust,
in the night of the banana leaves,

green ember,
hamadryad,

yakshi:

laughter in the brambles,
bundle of brightness in the thicket,

more music
than body,

more bird-flight than music,
more woman than bird:

your belly the sun,
sun in the water,

sun-water in the earthen jar,

sunflower seed I planted in my chest,
agate,

     ear of flame in the garden of bones.

For his funeral
Chuang-tzu asked heaven for its lights,

          the wind for its cymbals.

We asked the neem to marry us.
A garden is not a place:

     it is a passage,
a passion.

     We don't know where we're going,
to pass through is enough,

     to pass through is to remain:

BLISS

Peter Carey

HARRY JOY WAS TO DIE three times, but it was his first death which was to have the greatest effect on him, and it is this first death which we shall now witness.

There is Harry Joy lying in the middle of that green suburban lawn, beneath that tattered banana tree, partly obscured by the frangipani, which even now drops a single sweet flower beside his slightly grey face.

As usual Harry is wearing a grubby white suit, and as he lies there, quite dead, his blue braces are visible to all the world and anyone can see that he has sewn on one of those buttons himself rather than ask his wife. He has a thin face and at the moment it looks peaceful enough. It is only the acute angles struck by his long gangling limbs which announce the suddenness of his departure. His cheeks are slightly sunken, and his large moustache (a moustache far too big for such a thin face) covers his mouth and leaves its expression as enigmatic as ever. His straight grey hair, the colour of an empty ashtray, hangs over one eye. And, although no one seems to have noticed it, a cigarette still burns between two yellowed fingers, like some practical joke known to raise the dead.

Yet when the two fingers are burnt, he does not move. His little pot belly remains quite still. He does not twitch even his little finger. And the people huddled around his wife on the verandah twenty yards away have no justification for the optimistic opinions they shower on her so eagerly.

Harry Joy saw all of this in a calm, curious, very detached way. From a certain height above the lawn he saw the cigarette burning in his hand, but at the same time he had not immediately recognized the hand as his. He only really knew himself by

the button on his trousers. The lawn was very, very green, composed of broad-leaved tropical grasses, each blade thrillingly clear, and he wondered why everyone else had forsaken it for the shade of the verandah. Weeping came to him, but distantly, like short-wave signals without special significance.

He felt perfectly calm, and as he rose higher and higher he caught a fleeting glimpse of the doctor entering the front gate, but it was not a scene that could hold his interest in competition with the sight of the blue jewelled bay eating into what had once been a coastal swamp, the long meandering brown river, the quiet streets and long boulevards planted with mangoes, palms, flame trees, jacarandas, and bordered by antiquated villas in their own grounds, nobly proportioned mansions erected by ship-owners, sea captains and vice-governors, and the decaying stuccoed houses of shopkeepers. Around the base of the granite monolith which dominated the town, the houses became meaner, the vegetation sparser, and the dust rose from gravel roads and whirled in small eddies in the Sunday evening air.

Ecstasy touched him. He found he could slide between the spaces in the air itself. He was stroked by something akin to trees, cool, green, leafy. His nostrils were assailed with the smell of things growing and dying, a sweet fecund smell like the valleys of rain forests. It occurred to him that he had died and should therefore be frightened.

It was only later that he felt any wish to return to his body, when he discovered that there were many different worlds, layer upon layer, as thin as filo pastry, and that if he might taste bliss he would not be immune to terror. He touched walls like membranes, which shivered with pain, and a sound, as insistent as a pneumatic drill, promised meaningless tortures as terrible as the Christian stories of his youth.

He recognized the worlds of pleasure and worlds of pain, bliss and punishment, Heaven and Hell.

He did not wish to die. For a moment panic assailed him and he crashed around like a bird surrounded by panes of glass. Yet he had more reserves than he might have suspected and in a calm, clear space he found his way back, willed his way to a path beside a house where men carried a stretcher towards an ambulance. He watched with detachment whilst the doctor thumped the man on the chest. The man was thin with a grubby white suit. He watched as they removed the suit coat and connected wires to the thin white chest.

"My God," he thought, "that can't be me."

The electric shock lifted his body nine to ten inches off the table and at that moment his heart started and he lost all consciousness.

He had been dead for nine minutes . . .

He lived through thirty more wet seasons, seven droughts and two cyclones which happened, coincidentally, to have the same names as his new children.

So now there are only two stories left to tell, or rather two halves of the one story, and then it will all be done.

On the day of Harry Joy's death he was seventy-five years and two days old. He looked fifty. His face was deeply lined, you could even say creased, and it had been likened, by his children, to an old handbag. He walked with a slight limp, the result of a fall he suffered fighting a fire below the ridge at Clive's place. It was as close to a perfect day as might be possible, a warm sunny day in late October with the yellow box in flower and the "Yard" bees travelling out from their racks (necessary to protect them from cane toad) out through the canyons and canopies of Harry Joy's forest.

He had only come out to look at the blossom, nothing more, but he walked amongst the trees like a true gardener and even removed a piece of groundsel weed he judged had no right to be there. Down below in the valley he could hear Dani singing.

Nothing will happen in this story, nothing but a death. It is as inconsequential as anything Vance told. Soon the branch of a tree will fall on him. A branch of a tree he has planted himself, one of his precious yellow boxes, a variety prized by bee-keepers but known to forest workers as widow-makers (widder-makers) because of their habit, on quiet, windless days like this one, of dropping heavy limbs.

Any moment this thirty-year-old tree is going to perform the treacherous act of falling on to the man who planted it, while bees continue to gather their honey uninterrupted on the outer branches.

There—it is done.

There is nothing pretty in this last death, this split head, this broken life. There was nothing beautiful in the cracking cry of Honey Barbara as it later resounded around the valley, swept and swooped like a great panicked crow in a glass cage, like jet-black dove wings, the flapping overhead of flying foxes in the night.

But now the last story, and the last story is our story, the story of the children of Harry Joy and Honey Barbara, and for this story, like all stories, you must give something, a sapphire, or blue bread made from cedar ash.

He was dead, the yellow box branch across his head and arm, bees still collecting from the scanty blossom. He felt perfectly calm, and as he rose higher he could see Daze bringing the Clydesdale down the valley to where his grown-up children were dropping logs. He could see trees, trees he could name, and touch. Their leaves stroked him like feathers, eucalypt graced with mint, rose, honey, violet, musk, smells, came to him. He was in a place he had been in before. His nostrils were assailed with the smell of things growing and dying, a sweet fecund smell like the valleys of rain forests. He did not wish to return to his body and instead he spread himself thinner, and thinner, as thin as a gas, and when he had made himself thin enough he sighed, and the trees, those tough-barked giants exchanging one gas for another, pumping water, making food, were not too busy to take this sigh back in through their leaves (it took only an instant) and they made no great fuss, no echoing sigh, no whispering of branches, simply took the sigh into themselves so that, in time, it became part of their tough old heart wood and there are those in Bog Onion who insist you can see it there, on the thirty-fifth ring or thereabouts of the trees he planted: a fine blue line, they insist, that even a city person could see.